OPEN MIKE

A GOLDEN GARDENS MYSTERY

RENOIR

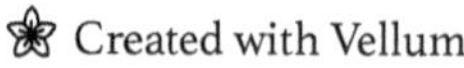 Created with Vellum

For Meredith - my darling bride and Muse

CONTENTS

1

You knew it was a miserable wet day in Dunbar when there was only one vehicle in the car park at the lookout over Cemetery Beach. It was one of the best whale watching spots in the district, and ordinarily in peak season there'd be a steady succession of sightseers at the popular spot. Not today, though. The rain was heavy and persistent, if not quite constant. Some low-lying parts of the town were underwater as the rain came down and the tidal creeks came up. Most everyone, tourist and local alike, had enough sense or self-preservation to keep themselves and their cars as close to home as possible.

One of the few exceptions was the white station wagon belonging to Arthur Bayer, which occupied *the* best vantage point of the lookout. The absence of competition and crowds had been a big part of the attraction of coming out this afternoon. The view over Cemetery Beach was one of the favourite things of Arthur's mother-in-law, Cailleach Steele (known universally as Callie, as so few people could pronounce her Gaelic name correctly).

Callie liked to be driven up to the lookout at least once per week. The whales may be seasonal, but there was plenty else to watch. Dolphins. Sharks. Boats, large and small. Birds, from seagulls to sea eagles. Interesting cloud formations. On a really quiet day, even the rhythm of the waves rolling in could be a pleasant diversion. All to be enjoyed from the comfort of the car, with a coffee, a cake, and the good company of Arthur and his wife, Callie's beloved daughter, Cianawyn Lauder.

The opportunity of enjoying the prime viewing spot in the car park had been too good to miss, as far as Callie was concerned. She was confident that there would be breaks in the weather during which it would be easier to look out through the windscreen. The wildlife, especially the sea critters, were wet anyway, so likely to be undeterred by the rain. And so it proved.

The sky was still leaden with dark clouds, but there were gaps between the regular heavy showers. Gaps when the windscreen could be cleared to open up the view out to sea. Intervals long enough, even, for Cianawyn and Arthur to get out of the wagon and stretch their legs with a stroll around the car park. Meanwhile Callie kept her feet warm and dry in the front passenger seat.

It was in the course of one such perambulation that Cianawyn leaned on the safety fence and looked down to where the waves rolled onto the narrow strip of sand at the base of the lookout cliff - a view not possible from the shelter of the car. In such weather, the waves didn't so much roll in as crash, but that could still made for interesting viewing.

Her brow creased, and she peered harder at the scene below.

"Ay!" she called to her husband, who was dumping a handful of coffee cups and cake wrappers in a convenient bin. "Come and take a look. What do you reckon that is? Some kind of big fish?"

She pointed down at a white shape near the water's edge, its details obscured by the surf's foam. Just as Arthur arrived at her side, a larger wave tumbled the object onto the shore.

Grasping his wife's arm, he answered, "That's no fish, Shan. I think that's a man. Or at least, it was."

A man who, it seemed, had two characteristics of certain fish. He'd been in the ocean, and he'd been gutted.

"I'll try to get him up the beach, so he doesn't get dragged back out by another wave. You look after your Mum, please."

Callie hadn't seen the body, but she saw the reactions of the other two clearly enough. Cianawyn had gone very pale, as had Arthur before he ran off. Well, 'ran' was too strong a word. He was slightly the other side of sixty from his darling bride, and running was only a memory for him. But he moved with longer than usual strides to the narrow staircase that had been bolted onto the cliff to take the keen and the confident to and from the beach below. It was the 'quick way', more direct but more harrowing than a track which wound down from the back of the car park to a point further along the sands, down the slope past the old pioneer graveyard which gave the beach its name.

Cianawyn got back into the wagon, sitting in the seat behind her mother.

"What's wrong, my girl? You look like you've seen a ghost."

"Where one might have come from, at least, Mum. It looks like a body washed ashore."

"Oh no – some idiot going out swimming in these conditions? Or fishing off the rocks?"

"I don't... think so. Most men don't fish nude. This didn't look like just a drowning..."

Realising that whatever her daughter had seen must have been distressing, Callie asked no more questions. They could happen later. The two women sat in silence, looking out and hoping that the rain didn't return in force while Arthur was on his way up or down the stairs. He wasn't keen on heights at the best of times, and it was a measure of how disturbing the sight must have been that he hadn't hesitated before rushing down the narrow structure.

There had been considerable public comment about the stairs when the Council had first installed them, years earlier – most of it negative. The main complaints were that they were unnecessary ("an eyesore", "environmental vandalism"), or inadequate ("that metal will rust", "too narrow").

The latter criticism had some validity. The stairway was barely the width of one-and-a-half average sized adults, so if a person or group was travelling up the stairs, and another coming down, there was a problem. One or other would have to go back up or down, or else try to squeeze past each other, edging between the cliff face and the waist-high handrail.

Fortunately, there was nobody else on the stairs, so Arthur made it down to the beach without being delayed by anything more than wet, slippery footing.

Seeing that the body was still in the shallows, but realising that it wouldn't be getting up and going anywhere, Bayer took the time to shed his deck shoes and roll the legs of his jeans up to the knee. Looking up, he was about to offer Cianawyn a reassuring wave, before realizing that she'd moved away from the edge of the lookout. Evidently, she'd taken his advice about sitting with Callie. Sensible.

From close range it was even more obvious that this was a very dead human male. Arthur had nursed some faint hope that this was perhaps a dummy or an inflatable, but known that they were unlikely options. Now, as he gripped a cold arm and started to haul the body in, using the incoming surf as much as possible, the truth was all too clear.

He tried to keep his eyes on the dead man's face. The blank stare was unpleasant, but preferable to the gaping wound that ran from sternum to groin. There was no blood – the sea water had evidently washed it clean – but the flesh hung loosely enough that bits of intestine and other viscera were disturbingly visible.

Soon enough, the body was out of the water. Without the assistance of the waves' action, the task of moving the dead weight was considerably more difficult. But with a determined effort, the corpse was dragged up the sand to a place close to the foot of the cliff. Even if Cianawyn had been watching, it was doubtful she'd be able to see much, the view obstructed by the angle of the rockface.

Arthur squatted on the rain-wet sand, catching his breath. What now? Was the tide coming in or going out? Had he moved the body far enough? Reluctantly, he looked more closely at the corpse. What had happened? Naked – by choice, or accident, or something more sinister? The death certainly didn't look accidental, although that could be possible, he supposed. The edges of the long wound were uneven, more like it had been torn than cut. There seemed to be no blood left. Presumably the sea was responsible for that. The face was pale enough to be bloodless, but maybe that was a result of death, or drowning, or just prolonged immersion. Arthur didn't have much experience with corpses, and even less with ones rolling in from the ocean.

The face – did that tell him anything? Eyes closed, mouth open. It wasn't familiar, but that meant nothing. There were over 4000 people in Dunbar, ten times that in the overall Shire. Obviously, Arthur didn't know most of them, even just by sight. And if the dead man had been an out-of-towner, well, just say that Bayer would have been much more surprised if he *had* recognised the dead face.

"Is everything alright there, mate?"

The unexpected voice behind him jolted Bayer out of a reverie he hadn't realised he'd slipped into. Turning, he saw two men clambering out of a small 'tinny' – an aluminium dinghy, about three metres long. He'd been so distracted he'd neither seen nor heard it glide in from the surf, the outboard motor off and the boat propelled by the waves.

Both were well wrapped up in wet-weather gear. One man was large, possibly well-muscled in his youth, but now more fat than fit. He had dark curly hair that was receding back over his forehead. Beside him was a much smaller fellow, wisps of blonde hair and a beard visible from under a large yellow rain hat. It was he who'd spoken.

"Saw you as we were going past – looked like you were struggling to drag something up the beach," he said.

Arthur nodded. "You were right," he replied, and indicated the gruesome find.

The curly-haired man made a peculiar pout, but his companion gave a low whistle and stepped forward.

"Looks nasty," he said, with a shake of his head.

"You're not kidding," Bayer agreed. "Saw him rolling in on the waves and thought I'd better try to get him in to dry land. Well, dry-ish, given the weather. Out of the surf, anyway, then ring the police."

"And what did they say?"

"I haven't called them yet. Came down those blasted stairs in such a rush, I didn't realise until I was down here that I'd left my phone in the car."

"Oh, that's a damned nuisance! Listen, don't worry. Graeme here's got his phone with him – we'll call 000 for you."

As the blonde man spoke, the rain started to re-intensify. It had eased from a light drizzle to an occasional brief splatter, but now the drops were getting larger and more frequent again.

The small man laid a reassuring hand on Arthur's arm. "Don't worry. We'll call them, and wait here till they arrive. We've got wet weather gear in the boat, we'll be fine. You'll get drenched otherwise."

Arthur looked ruefully skywards. "That damned staircase was slippery enough coming down..." he muttered.

"That settles it, then. Safety first. You get yourself back up as quickly as you safely can, eh? This poor chap's not going anywhere, and neither will we till he's properly taken care of."

The big man's expression hadn't changed much, bottom lip still protruding unhappily. The two boatmen huddled in their protective gear, and sat on rocks at the base of cliff.

"If the coppers ask who found the body, my name's Arthur. Arthur Bayer. My number is..."

"Oh, don't worry," the bearded man interrupted. "No need for you to even be involved. Dealing with the police about these things can be more trouble than it's worth. Never a 'thanks', only an endless stream of questions. We'll just explain that we noticed the body in the surf as we were cruising by."

Past experience had left Arthur with a jaded view of the Police Force as an institution, although there were a small number of indi-viduals he quite liked, so he impulsively agreed with the new arrival's suggestion.

A brief handshake – one only, the large man referred to as Graeme didn't so much as make eye contact – and Bayer headed back up the metal staircase as quickly as possible. By the time he reached the cliff-top the rain was getting heavy, and he didn't spare time for a backward glance as he hurried across the car park to the white station wagon.

As he jumped into the driver's seat and quickly shut the door, Callie looked at him with concern.

"Are you alright, dear boy? You're soaked," she said.

"Less soaked than I would be if I'd taken any longer coming back up those stairs!" her son-in-law replied with feeling.

As if to add emphasis to his words, the percussion of the rain on the wagon's roof suddenly got louder, making further conversation impossible. Both Callie and Cianawyn were understandably frustrated by this, especially when Arthur immediately turned the ignition key and headed for home. But there was little they could do until the drumming abated, which it failed to do all the way back to Golden Gardens.

Golden Gardens Retirement Estate was billed as a "welcoming community for the Over-55s" on the northern side of Dunbar. It was an attractive place on a patch of reclaimed swamp, which meant that under certain weather conditions the 300+ residents had to share the property with a much larger number of mosquitos. It seemed very likely that this would be the case again when the current spell of rain was over.

Golden Gardens was home to all three of the family: Cianawyn and Arthur in a two-bedroom bungalow on Peony Row, Callie occupying a room in the Emerald wing of Cromwell House, the on-site Permanent Care section of the Estate.

The weather meant that few of the Estate's residents were out and about, and there were even less visitors around than usual, so Arthur was able to park on Camellia Row right outside the main entrance to Cromwell House. With the aid of a large, bright blue umbrella, Cianawyn and Arthur were able to extract a collapsible wheelchair from the back of the wagon and convey the older woman into shelter without her getting wet.

It wasn't that Callie couldn't move without the chair, but it was quicker and easier for everyone if she used the aid. Her arthritis had become quite severe in the last two decades of her eighty-odd years, and although she made some effort to exercise by walking the corridors of Cromwell to visit other 'inmates' (the place bore the nickname 'Cromwell Penitentiary' among some residents), her mobility was declining.

The rain was still audible inside the building, but at least conversation was possible, and both women were bursting with questions.

"Not out here," said Arthur quietly as they crossed the Reception Foyer. All three smiled and waved to Victoria behind the front desk. She was one of the few regular occupants of that position who spoke English as their first language, and Arthur felt strangely reluctant to share his story outside the family just yet.

Soon enough, they were comfortably settled in Callie's room, the women in armchairs, Arthur sitting cross-legged on the bed. He took his time explaining what had happened earlier: his actions; the condition of the body, in detail more clinical than graphic; a description of the face, which was just as unfamiliar to his wife and mother-in-law; and the arrival and assistance of the two strangers in the small dinghy.

"I'm sorry about the phone," said Cianawyn, "I only noticed it in the console well after you'd gone. I could hardly drop it down to you."

"It's okay, Shan, I'm the one who forgot it. But the blonde guy seemed a very level-headed, dependable sort of bloke. I'm sure he'll have taken care of things and informed the coppers."

Which just goes to show that Arthur Bayer was a fair judge of character, but in no way prescient.

.ooo.

2

Two days later, the weather had improved only slightly.

Cianawyn and Arthur were again visiting Cailleach in Cromwell House. They were sitting in the common room, playing canasta with Charlie Royle, one of the other residents.

Charlie lived in the 'Amethyst' section of the Permanent Care Facility, meaning he was classed as "ambulatory but frail". Callie was in 'Emerald' – "impaired movement but lucid". The other sections were 'Opal' for palliative care, and 'Garnet' (officially the High Care Unit) for those residents colloquially (if unkindly) called "ga-ga".

Many of the Cromwell 'inmates' mingled readily and happily, within the Facility, out in the wider environs of Golden Gardens, or even in Dunbar and beyond. There were some who preferred the solitude of their room, and a small number who were confined to their room for their own safety and that of others. Those latter few could be found in Garnet if anyone outside the medical and support staff wanted to.

Among the willing 'minglers', Charlie was a familiar and popular figure. He was a lean man of 72 years. He'd played tennis until his late sixties, when worsening osteoporosis had left him too vulnerable to serious injury if he slipped or stumbled. He was charming, and loved a good conversation – especially with a member of the opposite sex, whatever their age. And it should be said, those conversations were seldom unwelcome. Charles had an old-fashioned upbringing, was unfailingly courteous, dressed and groomed himself neatly, and was well-read enough to chat about a wide range of topics.

His politeness extended beyond women. He was an experienced and very shrewd canasta player, but realised that Arthur was still new to the game, and played well within himself for the sake of the novice. Callie recognised and respected that – she was fond of her son-in-law, and appreciated his efforts to learn the rules and tactics so as to be involved in a pastime she enjoyed.

Nonetheless, she smiled broadly as she tapped her pen on the notepad on the table in front of her and said, "That takes us up to 1700. Well won, Charles."

"And a good effort by the youngsters," responded Royle, smoothing back his white hair.

The description was a bit cheeky, given that Arthur was less than ten years his junior and Cianawyn a few years younger than that. But it was said with good humour and obvious sincerity.

"Sorry, Shan," said Arthur quietly.

"Not a problem, Ay," she replied with a smile. "You did okay. You're not born knowing all the strategies, and I had Mum teaching me for years. Another game, honey?"

"Fine by me, if our veteran opponents are up to it."

The two men shared a smile and a wink at the gentle riposte.

"Only if someone furnishes this old lady with a cup of coffee," answered Callie with mock primness.

The common room was equipped with a machine that produced decent quality hot beverages for fifty cents per cup. The coffee wasn't barista class, but the price was a fraction of what would be paid in any of Dunbar's coffee shops.

Knowing the usual way of things, Cianawyn had brought with her a small purse full of coins. She extracted the requisite amount for a round of drinks. Arthur held out his palm, wordlessly offering to do the fetching and carrying.

With a smile and a shake of her head, she said, "You've only got two hands, honey, and those flimsy cups just might be hot this time. I'll come with you and help."

The couple strolled over to the machine in the corner and began the process of obtaining two cappuccinos with no sugar (the women), a flat white coffee with two (Arthur), and a white tea with one (Charles). As they waited for the machine to do its thing, they looked around the room idly. There were quite a few people present. Residents telling each other the same stories they'd told a dozen times before; families and other visitors recounting news of other people scarcely remembered or never even met; young staff gamely trying to converse with residents on a totally different wavelength; and one or two solitary folks staring silently into space, wrapped up in their own little world.

Arthur gave a friendly wave to one of those folks – a hulking man of Mediterranean appearance. Toni Torino, to use the professional name he much preferred, was a retired professional wrestler. It was a matter of some debate as to whether his apparent mental slowness was a result of age, degenerative illness, or too many blows to the head during his working life.

In fact, Arthur was quite sure that Toni wasn't as intellectually damaged as he seemed. An old wrestling fan himself, he'd enjoyed quite a few quiet conversations with the ex-matman about 'the business', and knew that Torino simply preferred not to interact much with other people. In this instance, though, the burly heavyweight at least gave a nod and a wave in reply, with a discreet smile thrown in.

"You're one of the only people I've seen give him the time of day, hon. And vice versa," observed Cianawyn.

Her husband smiled. "I'm a fan. I was really pleased to meet him, said so, and we got to talking. A lot of folks over the years have treated him, and his old mates, as meatheads - so he's just sort of... withdrawn."

Cianawyn nodded understandingly as she handed the cappuccinos to him, and turned to make the flat white.

Before he took so much as a step towards their table, Arthur frowned. He was looking at two men who'd just entered the common room. By their actions and movements, they were clearly a father and son, although the only evident physical resemblance was dark curly hair, greying on the older man. Both appeared to be damp with rain or sweat, or a combination of both.

"I know that face," Arthur said. The frown reflected his irritation at himself for not being able to identify the younger man.

"Hm?" Cianawyn turned, her own eyes following the direction of his gaze. "Oh! Hello, Sergeant!" she called.

The penny dropped for Arthur. The vaguely familiar face was out of context without a police uniform under it. Sergeant Chris Derbishire had been a visitor to their bungalow on Peony Row (more often than any of the three had liked) during the investigation of a mysterious death in Golden Gardens. Another instance of Arthur chancing upon a corpse, in fact. The sergeant's quiet, polite professionalism had endeared him to the family, especially for the contrast to the belligerent approach of Detective Sergeant Bob Sterling.

The younger of the two new arrivals looked over, smiled and waved. He gently took his older companion's arm and led him towards the couple.

"I'm off duty, Ms. Lauder. Please call me Chris."

"And we're Cianawyn and Arthur, right?" she replied.

"Yes, ma'am," was the young policeman's cheeky reply. "This is my Dad. We're moving him in today."

"Well! Welcome to Cromwell, Mr. Derbishire," exclaimed Cianawyn, extending her hand.

"If he's Chris, then I'm most definitely Kenneth," said the older man with a smile, as he shook the proffered hand.

Father and son accepted an offer to get coffee and join the canasta players at their table, where introductions were made all round. Callie had met the young sergeant briefly during what had turned out to be the murder investigation. She too had been impressed by his politeness and quiet efficiency.

When this was mentioned, Kenneth fairly glowed with pride. "I'm very pleased to hear that, Cailleach," he said, managing a reasonable job of the unfamiliar Gaelic pronunciation. "He's a third-generation copper, and we go back to a time when the job was held in more regard than it is now."

Arthur bit his tongue. His own experiences had made him deeply cynical about police in general, and meeting good ones genuinely surprised him. Both his wife and mother-in-law knew his views, and gently tried to deflect the conversation.

"So, Kenneth, what's led you to join us here?" asked the older woman.

The retiree sighed. "Rather gotten past the point of looking after myself, unfortunately. I've lived alone for over ten years, since Chris' Mum passed away, but I'm told that I'm now 'a falls risk', and I'm afraid I have to admit it's true. Don't like to say so out loud, though."

Charles nodded sympathetically. He'd only been on the periphery of the recent investigation, with minimal police contact, but both Derbishire men were likeable, and Charlie Royle was a gregarious fellow. "You'll doubtless be told that it's macho pride," he said in a mock conspiratorial tone.

Kenneth laughed. "Probably! I can get around alright by myself if I'm careful, so they've put me in Amethyst for the ambulatory. For now, at least. The old spine is deteriorating, though, so I'll probably be moving to Emerald eventually."

"Ah, then you'll become the lovely Callie's neighbour, whereas for now, alas, you're stuck with me down the hall. Sorry, old chap," said Royle.

"Well, it will be nice, if ironic, to have a policeman here in the Penitentiary," said Callie.

The older Derbishire looked puzzled, but smiled when the nickname of his new accommodation was explained to him. "It's not the most attractive building in the Estate, I must admit," he said.

It was something of a soapbox issue for Cianawyn. "The place is called Golden Gardens, but in reality, the best of the gardens are those maintained by the residents. In the common areas, and around Cromwell, it's left to the Estate staff, supposedly under the watchful eye of Syd Barrow."

"Beefy bloke? Met him. Seemed... full of himself," said Kenneth.

"Full of a lot of things," replied Cianawyn fiercely. Husband of the General Manager, Syd was something of a Lothario and liked trying out his 'chat-up' lines on the younger women of Golden Gardens, of whom she was one. No amount of blunt rejections seemed to deter him. Only that afternoon he'd made an inappropriate comment about her rain-wet shirt as he trundled past in the golf cart he used to get around the Estate.

Callie decided that a quick change of topic was in order. "If it's not too impertinent a question, Kenneth, what *is* the matter with your spine?" asked Callie, her active Curiosity Reflex piqued.

"A degenerative condition with a name about sixteen letters long. I've a very strong hunch that it's a long-term effect of an incident – let's be honest, a fight – when I was on the beat many years ago. I did try to claim compo for it, but the medical officers said there was at least as good a chance it was the result of an old footy injury. And I guess that's true."

"What code?" asked Arthur, who would watch any type of football (or, indeed, many other sports) if given the opportunity.

Derbishire Senior grinned. "The Greatest Game Of All. Rugby league, of course! Not to great heights, admittedly. A few Reserve Grade games for North Sydney, but never made First Grade. Work got in the way a bit, then a scrum collapsed on me, took me out for a while. I suppose that might be what did my back in," he admitted.

"Canasta is rather more sedate than rugby league, but do you play?" asked Cianawyn.

"Oh, sedate works for me, these days," he laughed. "Yes, I do play a bit. More of a poker man, but I can enjoy any card game."

"If you'd like a game now, and my beloved doesn't mind, you can sit in for me. You can't be a worse partner than I am," offered Arthur.

"Only at cards, my love," his wife replied. "And you are getting better, you know. But certainly, if you're interested, Kenneth, you're welcome."

The Derbishires looked at each other. Chris shrugged, but Kenneth shook his head.

"No," the older man said. "We have to finish unpacking the car and getting my room set up. And no," he continued, forestalling his son's objection even as Chris opened his mouth, "I don't intend to let you do it on your own, lad."

"I could help, while you..."

"Thanks, but no, Arthur. My stuff, my responsibility. I might be less help than I'd like to be these days, but I'll still do my bit. The outside stuff is mostly done anyway, so we'll be out of the rain while I figure out how I want the room set up."

Kenneth was adamant, so when their coffees were finished (which didn't take long – for 'safety reasons' the machine was programmed to produce water less hot than most people wanted it) father and son politely took their leave.

"Nice chaps, the pair of them," said Charles approvingly, once the game had recommenced.

"Indeed," Callie agreed. "I look forward to seeing more of Mr. Derbishire Senior around the place.

"Gasp! Don't say I have competition for your affections!" exclaimed Royle in feigned shock.

Cailleach looked at him blankly. "No, that's not a thing I'm likely to say."

A poker face is useful in canasta, too.

Soon after, Arthur leaned across the table and quietly said to his partner, "Do you think I should have asked the sergeant – Chris – about that body on the beach?"

"No, hon," was the soft but emphatic reply. The grisly discovery hadn't been mentioned to Charlie, and there seemed no good reason to do so now. "Chris is off duty, and more to the point, he has quite enough on his mind right now."

"Fair enough. I'm sure it's all been sorted out by now, and there's nothing for anyone to worry about."

As previously noted, Arthur Bayer had no talent for predicting the future.

.ooo.

3

It was the Tuesday evening after Kenneth Derbishire's arrival in Cromwell House. Cianawyn and Arthur were settling into their station wagon, preparing to head out to the far side of Dunbar. Specifically, to the Terrence Community Theatre.

The old village of Terrence was long gone. It had become an outer suburb of Dunbar, as the coastal town's population had slowly swollen. Eventually, even the name had fallen off the maps. Commemorating an old writer was felt to be less important than recognising the earlier Indigenous inhabitants of the region, so the suburb was called Goonambilli. The old wooden hall, converted into a playhouse in the 1950s, was the last place to retain the Terrence name.

"I'm still not entirely sure about this, Shan..."

"You'll be fine, sweetheart. It's not a big role, and Dolly has promised that you won't have to sing. Not that there's anything wrong with your singing, but I know you'd rather do blues or rock than music hall, and *Sweeney Todd, The Musical* is very definitely a vaudeville style show, musically anyway."

"With Dolly Bertram as Musical Director, it couldn't be anything else, I suppose. Are we swinging by her townhouse to pick her up?" asked Arthur, backing out of the garage.

"Not this time. She had things to do in town first, apparently. But if this works out, it'll make sense to car pool in future."

"Mm."

Arthur sounded uncertain, and so he was.

Dolly had been retired and living in Golden Gardens for several years, but in her younger days she'd been an active, and successful, singer and dancer. In truth, she was capable of quite a range of styles, but her first love was comedy, especially the old music hall variety of the 1920s and '30s. She'd often lament that she'd born "just a few decades too late, luvvy". She still played piano to entertain the residents, and to reach a wider audience she'd become involved in the Dunbar & District Players, the resident company in the Terrence Community Theatre.

Occasionally dramatic, the DDP more usually specialised in 'light entertainment'. The latest musical was one such offering. Knowing that Cianawyn Lauder had an interest in period clothing, and liked spending time with her sewing machine and some interesting fabric, it hadn't required too much effort to enlist a new wardrobe designer for the show.

And Cianawyn had found that she was rather enjoying the challenge of designing, sourcing, upcycling and sewing the Dickensian style of outfits required. It wasn't such a great imposition, she'd found. Indeed, she'd only attended two rehearsals, and hadn't even met nearly half of the cast yet. She'd met the show's director, of course – the imposing but good-natured Shauna Shallacot. Shauna hadn't rushed her – there was plenty of time before *Sweeney* was to open.

That turned out to be just as well, because the fellow cast as the leading man, the melodrama villain of the play's title, had suddenly stopped turning up to rehearsal. No explanation, no contact, not answering his phone, messages unanswered. So, another of the men in the cast had been 'promoted' into the lead, but that left a vacancy. The Players had plenty of women amongst their membership, but not a lot of males. Certainly not males who were available, or even remotely suitable for the role.

Dolly had had a flash of inspiration. She knew Arthur could carry a tune, better than he admitted. He was about the right age, or could pass for it without too much make-up. And with Cianawyn already involved in the show, some additional leverage could be applied.

The upshot of all of which was that Arthur Bayer was now on his way to his first rehearsal as Colonel Eustace Jeffrey, formerly of the British Army in India, and loyal friend to Johanna Oakley (the sweet young heroine) and her beau Mark, presumed to be a victim of the murderous barber Todd.

Yes, he was uncertain. He knew melodrama wasn't exactly the pinnacle of classical acting, but was deeply unsure of his own ability to remember lines. He struggled with names, phone numbers and dates, so how on earth was he to cope with dialogue and cues? But (inveigled by Dolly), his beloved Shan had convinced him he would be more than capable. Even allowing for her innate bias, he didn't think he would be "great", as suggested, but he didn't want to disappoint his darling, either.

"Apparently, it's quite a blow, losing the original lead like this," said Cianawyn as they travelled. "Not just the casting chaos, but he was going to be good for publicity."

"How so?"

"It was Mike Salmon. The morning announcer on the local radio station. The proverbial 'prominent local identity'. He'd have brought some fans in, or that was the thinking."

Community Radio Dunbar – CRD-FM as it was called (less flatteringly, Radio Crud to its critics) operated with a small transmitter which didn't project much past the environs of the town itself. Oddly enough, it could be picked up further out to sea than on land, and was popular with the boating and fishing fraternity. Staffed by volunteers in all but the senior management positions, it had a substantial, and loyal, local following.

Arthur frowned. "Odd that a bloke in such a public position would just quit suddenly. He must know it's bound to generate some negative feeling. But hang on, surely he can be contacted through the station?"

"Apparently, he's not turned up there, either, Dolly says. Gordon Teller has been doing his shift for a few days."

"Gordon? Well, that should cheer him up!"

"You know him?" asked Cianawyn, surprised.

"Kind of. We're both fond of the coffee at the Flying Saucer. We struck up a conversation one day, and now, well, we'll share a table and a chat if we happen to both be there."

"Ah. 'Cheer him up', you said?"

Arthur smiled. "Gordon isn't the cheeriest of blokes. He's got a long list of grievances against the world. High on that list, usually, is his treatment at CRD-FM. He's been on their volunteer announcers' list for years, but only ever gets fill-in jobs when somebody's sick or unavailable. Never been so much as offered his own spot, at any time of the day or night. Frustrates the hell out of him, because he really can't work out why."

"Have you any idea why?"

"I just assume he's said something to put someone's nose out of joint, somewhere along the way. He's not backward about coming forward with his opinions, and if he's in a grumpy mood he can be – undiplomatic."

Cianawyn nodded. "We should tune in one morning. It might be interesting to hear what your friend is like."

"Sure. Can't be worse than the one or two times I caught the missing guy, Salmon. All forced jollity and 'It's me, your best pal' sort of nonsense. What was he like as an actor?"

"I've no idea. He's one of the ones I haven't met yet. We'll have to ask Shauna. Not that it matters, if he's flitted off somewhere. Truth to tell, I don't think she minds losing Mike. When it comes to directing, she's a bit 'my way or the highway', and I gather he tended to do things a bit... differently. Every time."

"She's – tough?"

"She can be, if required, I think. You'll have to decide for yourself. I think Shauna is nice – jolly, even, sometimes. She and Dolly can, by turns, be best buddies or butt heads, so don't let our dear musical director influence you one way or the other!"

The rest of the journey was spent discussing the play itself – what they'd read, and the few scenes that Cianawyn had seen at the two rehearsals she'd attended.

As arranged, they arrived at the Terrence Theatre a little early, so Arthur would have the chance to meet his director, and vice versa.

Shauna Shallacot was quite a short woman, with a build that could fairly be called barrel-shaped. She worked hard at being genial, but it was clear that she had a forceful, and formidable, personality. Just as Cianawyn had done a few weeks earlier, Arthur found himself immediately liking her, but also feeling a little daunted. Upsetting Shauna would <u>not</u> be a wise move.

"Well," she said, pushing a few stray long hairs from her face, "I reckon you'll make a quite different Colonel Jeffrey to Alan Strong. Older, for one thing. But that's okay. He's certainly a different Sweeney to what Mike was. He's actually managing to make the villain almost likeable at times."

Arthur nodded. "Not many villains or crooks actually see themselves as such, I reckon. Misunderstood, put upon, victimised, or even morally 'in the right'. Not many folks would see themselves as evil in the way that others do."

"Good point. Makes a character more well-rounded and believable, even in a melodrama. Now, Cianawyn, let's talk costumes…"

So, Arthur sat quietly trying to learn lines while his beloved and the director discussed details of Dickensian styled costumes for characters rich and poor.

The cast required for that evening's rehearsal soon began arriving. First was Angelika Judd – tall, young, with long black hair and the sort of big dark eyes that painters adore. She was an ideal choice for Johanna, the romantic female lead.

She'd barely introduced herself when her stage 'father' arrived. Darryl Frankem was a small man, with some silver in his blonde hair and beard. As he shook Arthur's hand, the new cast member noticed a spatter of blood on the cuff of the shorter man's white shirt.

Angelika noticed the same thing, and gave a little cry of "Ooh!" She laid a hand on Frankem's arm and asked, "Darryl, are you okay?"

"Eh? Oh. My sleeve. Yeah, yeah, I'm fine, thanks. Had to do a bit of late surgery on a dog, and I didn't have time to go home and change shirts. Sorry if it upsets you, Angelika. Or you, Arthur," he said apologetically.

"Oh, I'm alright, thanks. Just concerned about you," replied the actress. "Darryl's a vet, when he's not playing my Dad."

Bayer raised an eyebrow. "At the Clinic a few doors down from the Flying Saucer? I thought I vaguely recognised you from somewhere..."

"No, no, I've got a private practice. My clients are nearly all in the racing industry. I'm kept busy enough there without people's pets."

Just then, Dolly Bertram, who was portraying Darryl's wife, arrived. Dolly was a larger than life personality who could dominate a room without even trying. She strode around the room dispensing hugs and cheery greetings. The last embraces were saved for Cianawyn and Shauna.

"Right then," said the director. "Cianawyn, I'm going to assume you know your husband's measurements, or else can discover them readily enough." A giggle went around some of the performers. "We've got the whole Oakley family here – can you get all their measurements, please? Let's think about how we want them to look. I'd like some sort of commonality between all three."

"To reinforce their being related, but a bit subtly," mused Cianawyn. "The same fabric, or a matching pattern, might be a bit too obvious. Similar shades of colours, maybe?"

"Yes, that's what I had in mind."

"Green for oak leaves, brown for oak wood," offered Arthur, who loved a pun.

Shauna nodded. "Brown might be a bit sombre, especially for Johanna, but the right shade of green could work."

"A dress for Johanna, maybe a hat or a shawl for her Mum, and a vest for Dad? So that the colour's there, but not too 'in your face' on the parents," suggested the seamstress.

"Yes," agreed the director. "In fact, I think we could make a theme of this. Villains in black, obviously – Sweeney, Mrs Lovatt, even that rogue Doctor Lupin – well, he's a reverend so it makes sense anyway. As to the others... well, I'll give it some thought, and call you in a couple of days, Cianawyn."

"Fine. I'll give it some thought, too," came the reply.

"Good, thanks. Right, until Will gets here, sorry Arthur – Will Marlowe is playing the lecherous, rum-swilling reverend Lupin. Until then, let's look at the Oakley family in Act 1, Scene 3. Colonel, you arrive bearing a message for Johanna from her lost love..."

Cianawyn settled into a seat near Shauna, so she could ask questions if required, and proceeded to enjoy the show. Even in this, its roughest form, she could see some flashes of cleverness. Not so much in the script, which was melodrama 'writ large', but in the casting. Angelika had Dolly's colouring and height, but was several sizes slimmer. Her stage father, Darryl, was appropriately slender, albeit more than a half-a-head shorter.

Smiling with quiet pride at her husband's obvious understanding of the quirky requirements of melodramatic acting, Cianawyn felt herself relaxing. *Sweeney Todd* would be fun, and other than the pressure of finishing costumes on time, should provide a few nice, stress-free weeks. For her, at least.

.ooo.

4

———————

Perhaps the most popular element of the whole Golden Gardens Estate was the 'clubhouse' and function room, and especially its small, well-stocked bar: The Watering Hole.

Every Friday evening it was the venue for the more sociable of the residents to get together for drinks at better prices than offered anywhere else in Dunbar. For many, it was a chance to swap both gossip and genuine news, as well as reminiscences and other tall tales.

Arthur was in his second week of rehearsals, and Cianawyn had finally met all of the cast and taken their measurements. They were at their regular table, with Dolly Bertram and Cianawyn's Mum, Callie, who they routinely conveyed from Cromwell on Fridays. At the table, also, were their friends Dawn Crane and Jim Cooke, two quiet residents who some folks erroneously assumed to be a couple. And joining them for the first time was Kenneth Derbishire, who'd accepted the invitation to share the ride with Callie.

Musical director Dolly was preening over how well rehearsals were progressing. "It's goin' lovely, ducks," she exclaimed. "The young folks are doin' us proud, and some of us older ones are goin' okay, too. If I do say so meself."

A smile and nod of agreement came from Cianawyn. "The girl who plays the young boy Tobias is very good. An interesting bit of casting. A nice touch from Shauna too, that the 'boy' and her best friend are African and Asian. Helps add to the sense of their isolation from the other characters. Even Tobias' mother isn't very dark, for all that Sophie Asquith has an Indigenous mother herself."

Dolly nodded. "The Asquith's is an old local family, Soph tells me. Been in these parts for generations, she reckons. Both sides of the family. Opposite of young Han Soo Thie. His folks only came a couple o' years ago, an' set up their restaurant. Lad can act though, and sing."

"That would be 'Thie's Thai', I suppose. I did wonder when I saw his name. Good kid, but we haven't spoken much," said Arthur.

"The tradition of boys playing female roles goes back to Shakespeare's day, of course," said Callie. "It's a nice switch to have a girl as a male."

"The part was written that way, luvvy. All the songs for the boy Tobias was meant for a soprano, and young Miracle's got the perfect voice," explained Dolly.

"Miracle? What an... interesting name!" exclaimed Jim.

Cianawyn smiled. "Miracle Agunwe, although that's not what you'll read in the program. She wants to be called 'Mary Adams'. She's from Eritrea originally – came here as a little girl, she wants to make her name as an Aussie, she says."

"Typical," said Arthur, without malice. "I've worked with her for nearly two weeks. You've met her once, to get her measurements, and you know her life story."

"We chatted, while I ran the tape measure over her. That's all," replied his wife. "People just talk to me. I get it from Mum. Miracle's a nice enough girl. Ambitious."

"Well, there's nothing wrong with that," observed Callie. "Provided the ambition isn't at the expense of common decency."

Her son-in-law grunted. "Yeah. Too often, the line between ambitious and ruthless gets crossed too easily. And sometimes, ambition exceeds ability."

"You sound as though you have someone in mind," said Dawn.

"A few people, actually," Arthur admitted with a wry smile. "That bloody Detective Sergeant we had to deal with a little while ago springs to mind."

"The lovely D. S. Sterling, yes, he made an impression," agreed Cianawyn.

That prompted a loud laugh from Kenneth Derbishire, though he quickly suppressed it.

"Sorry," he said. "I could tell you a few stories about Bob Sterling. He was just starting out in the Force when I was getting near the end of my career. I shouldn't tell tales out of school, though."

"Did you and your son serve at Dunbar station together?" asked Callie, between sips of wine.

"No, unfortunately not. His first posting was out west, then down south for a while. By the time he got sent here, I'd been gone for about six months, seeing out my time behind a desk in the Big Smoke. Hated it. If I'd had any thoughts of delaying my retirement, that job finished them."

Arthur scratched at his chin. Shauna had asked him to try to cultivate a beard for his role as Colonel Jeffrey, and it was just getting to the irritating, itchy stage.

"Thinking of Sergeant Chris, I wonder how he's gone with identifying that body we found. I'd hoped he might have let us know something, just out of curiosity," he said.

"Body?" said Kenneth, his own curiosity piqued.

Arthur made a discreet 'not now' signal. He suddenly realized that he'd not mentioned the grisly find to anyone but his immediate family. Golden Gardens was like a petri dish for gossip, especially on a Friday evening, and he had no wish to become a part of any fresh 'news-that-wasn't-news'.

Fortunately, only a minute or two later that Meg and John Piper arrived at the table, selling tickets for this evening's raffle. The Old Bastards charity, to which several of them belonged, had this as a regular fundraiser. Tonight's main prize was a $100 garden store voucher, only really useful to a few, but most folk regarded the purchase of tickets as a donation anyway. John managed his usual "Hello, thanks," as Arthur and Kenneth handed over $5 each. Meg, as ever, was willing and able to talk the leg off a billiard table and quickly had most of the group engaged in conversation.

That allowed Arthur a few minutes to quietly explain to Kenneth what had happened at the Cemetery Beach lookout.

The retired policeman looked thoughtful. "Chris hasn't mentioned it, and I'd expect he would," he said softly. "He tries to keep me informed on anything interesting locally, and that would fit into that category. I'll ask him next time I see him."

"Thanks," said Bayer. "It's not like I can do anything about it, but it's – an open loop, I guess."

"Understood. And I'll keep it quiet."

The pair exchanged nods and winks. The Derbishires may turn out to be the men to overcome Arthur Bayer's long-held deep bias against the police.

Jim stood, and coughed politely. "I'm going to the bar. Can I get anyone else anything while I'm there?"

As it happened, everyone at the table had finished, or almost finished, their drinks. That meant that Jim found himself with a substantial order. He wasn't expected to pay for it all, but it would be awkward to carry the whole lot.

"I'll give you a hand, mate," volunteered Arthur, standing.

After the two men had strolled away, Dawn surprised everyone by leaning forward conspiratorially and signalling to get their attention.

"I wonder if I might ask of all of you a favour, please?" she said quietly.

Nods and puzzled "Sure" mutterings rippled around the table.

Dawn smiled nervously. "I don't know if you were aware – I don't think he's said much about it – but Jim's taken on a new position. Not a job as such, but volunteering as a guide at the Fishing Museum."

Expressions of surprise around the table confirmed that Jim had, indeed, kept his news to himself.

Dawn continued. "I think he's quite nervous about it, and I

wondered if we perhaps might support him by going along and, well..."

"Being encouraging and enthusiastic," offered Cianawyn.

Dawn nodded gratefully. It had been one of the longest speeches any of them had heard her make, which was a measure of the depth of her friendship with Jim.

"It's a great idea! We can do that, I'm sure. What day?" asked Cianawyn, smiling broadly.

"He starts next Friday morning," replied Dawn, who was already glowing with a combination of embarrassment and pleasure at the reception she'd garnered.

"I confess to having no interest in fishing," admitted Callie. "I do, however, have an interest in history. I'd be happy to go along, if someone can offer transport."

"We can arrange that," said Cianawyn, which was exactly the response her mother expected.

"I'm certainly interested," agreed Kenneth. "I wonder, though, if it might be a bit overwhelming if we all turned up *en masse*?"

Cailleach nodded agreement. "Dawn, I'm sure you'd like to be there early for him." That won a shy but grateful nod. "Cian, if you and the boy could pick me up after morning tea, we could be at the Museum for elevenses. Dolly, might you be able to collect Kenneth a little closer to lunchtime?"

"Of course, ducks, if that suits everyone? What time is Jim working until?"

It was a measure of Callie's force of personality that everyone accepted her suggestion without demur.

"His shift is nine until one, I believe," said Dawn. "Thank you all so much – I... oh, look out, they're coming back!"

Jim and Arthur brought the drinks to the table, engrossed in their own conversation about the comparative merits of certain wines. They were both clearly oblivious to the others' planning.

Cianawyn picked up on the thread of their conversation and put in her own opinion, effectively guiding everyone at the table into waters well away from the Fishing Museum.

Like the others, she was fond of Jim. It was good to have something positive to look forward to, she thought.

.ooo.

5

———————

It had been a pleasantly uneventful weekend in Golden Gardens. Sadly, that didn't turn out to be the case in other parts of Dunbar.

Chris had been to visit his father on Sunday. During the course of their typically rambling conversation, Kenneth had recounted Arthur's story of the body he'd found washed up at Cemetery Beach. Chris had looked at him blankly and said that as far as he knew, no such report had come in, and even if it hadn't come to him directly, he would have seen something of that nature. He could swear with his hand on his heart that no such call had ever been received.

"Puzzling, though. I know Arthur, and he's not given to imagining things, far less making them up. Bob Sterling might not be so respectful…"

"I can imagine," agreed his father.

"I'll check into it on Monday," Chris said.

He hadn't forgotten that undertaking when he arrived at the station the following morning, but his intrigue had to be shelved when, as soon as he walked into the old building, he was excitedly informed by a young constable that a body had been found "on the beach".

But this wasn't at Cemetery Beach. The find had been made on Sunday, two beaches further along the coast, at the base of the imaginatively named High Point. The discoverer was an optimistic rock fisherman who'd been picking his way above the tide line. Looking for somewhere to set up for his morning's diversion, the fellow had stumbled upon a body, face down among the rocks. The clothes weren't even damp, so there seemed no chance it had washed ashore.

Initially, it had all the appearances of a suicide. High Point was a known trysting spot for couples of all genders and persuasions – the area around Dunbar wasn't big enough for 'straight' places and 'gay' places, so everyone seemed to get on with minding their own business in privacy.

Clearly there would have to be some investigation, and Chris would have a role in this. He was handed the case file by the Detective Sergeant Bob Sterling, together with a scant, twenty-second explanation. Fortunately, that was supplemented by a considerably more detailed briefing from Sterling's considerably more effective right-hand-person, Detective Rita Mulholland.

Sergeant Derbishire spent much of the rest of the day checking Missing Person reports from Dunbar and other stations up and down the coast. He didn't feel any need to see the body for himself. The coroner, Doctor Cartwright, had written her report with her usual attention to detail, and her description was enough for him to work from.

There were a few possible matches, but follow-up phone calls allowed him to progressively rule lines through all of them. Too tall, too young or old, obviously wrong physique, wrong skin colour, even in one case the wrong number of limbs.

The second-hand description of the Cemetery Beach body that he'd received from his father didn't seem to match, either. But nothing else had come up trumps, and the afternoon was waning. Out of respect to his father, and by extension, Arthur Bayer, Chris decided to end his working day with a visit to the latter. A few questions couldn't hurt, and even though a link seemed unlikely, he'd feel better for trying to close his Dad's open loop.

The policeman knew his way to the bungalow on Peony Row, from prior experience. He found Arthur in a shaded corner of the front garden, pruning a young grevillea bush.

After exchanging pleasantries, the young man was invited in for a cold drink while they talked about 'business'. Just as he'd done with the older Derbishire, Arthur recounted the incident in as much detail as he could recall.

"What did this man look like?"

"Dead. Very."

"A bit more detail, Mr. Bayer?"

Arthur gave as good a description as the circumstances, and his memory, would allow.

The Sergeant shook his head. "I'm sorry, Mr. Bayer. Based on what I'd already heard from my Dad, I checked the station records thoroughly. No Missing Persons reports of anyone resembling the description. There's no indication of having received any sort of report about anything like this. Whoever your two friends were..."

"Not friends. Not seen before, and not seen since," Arthur corrected.

"Okay. Whoever the two men were, it would seem that they didn't make the call that they promised they would."

Derbishire looked at the comprehensive notes he'd been making as Arthur talked. "I have to say, the body you described bears no resemblance to the body that was found on Sunday morning."

"What body's this?" asked Arthur.

Derbishire sighed. "Perhaps I shouldn't tell you this, but under the circumstances, sharing information may not hurt, and I do know I can trust you to keep it quiet for now. There was a corpse found at the base of High Point on the weekend. It completely doesn't match the description that you've just given me. The person in question was male, yes, but fully clothed, and as I understand it, didn't have anything like the sort of elongated torso wound that you've described. He was battered and broken in a way that would be consistent with a fall from the top of the cliff. Neither was there any sign of immersion in the water, certainly not the long-term signs you say you saw.

Furthermore, the body you described would seem to have been that of an older white male, yes?"

"I'd have said so. I guess water damage might have affected his appearance, but that's what I'd have taken him to be. Have been."

"Okay. The weekend's victim was in his twenties, and clearly a Pacific Islander, although we don't yet have details. Is there any chance you could have been mistaken? As I understand it, on the day you made the – ah – discovery, the weather conditions weren't good."

"No, no they weren't, but I can tell the difference between Caucasian and Polynesian. Even allowing for time in the sea, I don't reckon the skin I saw was ever dark."

"Hmm," mused Derbishire. "Puzzling. The best I can do, I'm afraid, Mr. Bayer, is to keep my notes and write an Incident Report. We can only wait to see what happens next. It'll be up to D. S. Sterling to decide what, if any, resources get put to an investigation."

"Perhaps best if you don't make my name too prominent then."

Derbishire grinned. "I can understand why you'd say that. You didn't get on terribly well last time, did you? But given the nature of the report, it'll be a bit hard to avoid."

"Well, that's that, then, hey?"

"I'll be as diplomatic as I can. Honestly, I'm not sure what resources the D. S. proposes putting to this new enquiry, far less investigating a body that we <u>don't</u> have."

If Detective Sergeant Bob Sterling possessed a more sensitive nature, his ears may have been burning as Bayer and Derbishire discussed him. As it was, his ears were no hotter than usual. Nothing about Sterling was more sensitive than usual. He was in conversation with Rita Mulholland regarding the body found at the base of High Point.

The D.S. sounded dismissive. "It's a pick-up spot, isn't it? Well, if not 'pick-up', a make-out spot anyway. Probably a jilted lover or a love affair gone wrong, something like that. The stupid bugger, in a fit of remorse, decided to throw himself off the cliff. Happens all the time. Maybe not around here, but in the grander scheme of things it's not uncommon. I don't see there'll be much for us to investigate here beyond identifying the deceased."

Mulholland looked at him uncertainly. "Are you sure, sir? There are at least one or two other possibilities, aren't there?"

Sterling raised irritated eyebrows. "Such as?"

"Well, as you say sir, it's a popular spot for couples. Maybe there was an argument."

"Between him and his girlfriend, you mean? Or perhaps boyfriend, given what I've heard about the spot. Mmm, possible," Bob conceded.

"Or maybe there was a jealous lover, or a jilted partner."

"And our dead guy could be the jilter or the jiltee," said Sterling, chuckling at his own dark humour.

"Or even," mused Rita, "given the nature of some of the couples known to frequent High Point, it could be a hate crime."

"Hmpf," Sterling snorted. "I suppose that's possible. Even understandable up to a point, I guess. Town like this isn't noted for its liberal thinking."

Not for the first time in her working life, Rita had to stifle an observation about the irony of her boss accusing anyone else of intolerance. Sterling wasn't exactly homophobic, he was an equal-opportunity misanthrope. He disliked most people, regardless of gender, colour, faith, sexual preference or what hand they wrote with.

Bob Sterling didn't lack imagination, it's just that his was a dark and unpleasant one that only seems to conjure up the worst in a situation or person. And once he'd had that idea, it was very hard to get him to let go of it, Rita Mulholland had observed.

And now, the Detective Sergeant's interest was suddenly piqued. The prospect of a murder investigation, especially one that may be a bit salacious (thus capturing some media attention), captured his ambitious eye. He still nursed the hope of recognition in more senior circles of the Force, and from that, promotion out of the backwater he felt Dunbar to be.

He'd hitherto paid minimal attention to what he'd thought of as a messy but otherwise mundane suicide, but as that dark imagination kicked in, he wondered if it might be a case with a higher profile, to bring some spotlight in his direction...

The Detective Sergeant sat a little straighter in his chair. He frowned at Rita. "Are we getting a coroner's report?"

"Of course, sir. The deceased has been with Doctor Cartwright – she's delivered a preliminary report. She's doing a more detailed examination now, and she's confident we'll have something soon."

"Digging deeper, eh?"

Rita treated the attempt at wit with a transparent smile, replying, "Something like that, sir. The cause of death looks straightforward enough."

Sterling offered his trademark grunt. "It seems that way. Consistent with a fall from the top of the cliff, pretty simple. Doesn't take too much imagination."

Rita made no comment aloud about the limits of his own imagination. "But the doctor's being thorough, as usual. That is her job. It would be a help, of course, if we knew the identity of the victim," said Rita.

"Be a good place to start," agreed her boss. "Check fingerprints. See if we can get a photograph that's recognizable. Not too grotesque, at least. Then start circulating it, especially round the Islander community. They all know each other. I take it you didn't recognize him?"

It was a measure of his own disinterest in the case up to that point that he hadn't even seen the corpse, despatching Mulholland and a couple of 'the uniforms' to look after the tedious standard procedures and messy details. She considered her reply.

"No, sir. It's not going to be an attractive photograph, but it may be enough for friends or family to recognize."

"Hmpf. That'll have to do, then. Damn shame if we upset someone, but that's an occupational hazard," he said primly.

Upsetting people had never bothered Bob Sterling.

"Be a good girl and go get me a coffee – that always helps me think. Make one for yourself, too," he added magnanimously.

"Thank you, sir," she replied with the scant courtesy of experience.

She knew it didn't fall within her Official Duties, but was a sacrifice worth making for a comparatively quiet life.

As she was returning from the tea room she was intercepted by one of the uniformed officers on duty.

"Detective Mulholland? This just arrived from the Coroner's Office for you," said the constable.

"Thanks," she said, allowing the young man to tuck the large envelope under her arm as she held a coffee in each hand.

Recognizing the awkwardness of her situation, the constable walked with her and helpfully opened the door to the Detective Sergeant's room. She gave the uniformed youngster a grateful nod as he retreated back to his desk.

"No biscuits?" asked Sterling peevishly as his cup was placed in front of him.

"No, sir. All out," she lied. "Something more useful, though, I hope."

She put the envelope on the desk, and extracted the file it contained. "I'm sorry, I haven't had time to look at it, far less read it, yet."

"Well," said Bob lugubriously through a mouthful of coffee, "we'll discover things together, won't we?"

He took the file from her hands with a quick movement that was just short of snatching the folder. As he opened it, though, his expression changed. His jaw fell open, and he stared, almost comically. Mulholland knew better than to laugh, though. Indeed, she was immediately concerned at the reaction.

"Sir?" she hazarded.

He was staring at the autopsy photograph atop the file. His detective was surprised. The cuts and bruises meant that it wasn't a pretty picture, but she was sure that he'd seen worse in his career?

Sterling's jaw worked soundlessly for a moment, before he was able to force out the words, "I know that face!"

"Really?" she asked in genuine surprise.

It took some moments for any further reply. The Detective Sergeant dropped the folder as if he'd just discovered it to be covered in fire ants.

"That's Solomona Tuafeulaki!" he exclaimed. "Plays second row for Dunbar footy club."

"The Rugby League team?"

"Yes, of course!"

Something in his voice gave her a clue. "You have some involvement with them, sir?"

He nodded. Rita was finding her boss's reaction difficult to read. He seemed puzzled, surprised, shocked and disappointed all at once.

"Do you – know the man, sir?"

Haltingly he explained that the dead man played in the first-grade side for the Dunbar Demons.

"And you…?" she prodded gently.

"Been a member for years, since I first came to Dunbar. Haven't played for quite a while. Kept my membership up when I stopped, though. Tried to stay involved a bit, as much as time allows. Solly is – was – a good bloke. News to me he had a girlfriend, though. Can't think what he'd be doing up at High Point. Doesn't make sense."

As he held the photo, staring uncomprehendingly, Rita slid the coroner's report from the folder and began to read. Her eyebrows raised.

She read, pondered, then carefully said to her supervising officer, "Sir, I don't want to disturb you, any further, but I think you should know this."

"What?"

"Doctor Cartwright has found evidence of drugs in Mr. Tuafeula-ki's system."

"What sort of drugs?"

"That's… not an easy question to answer. Not something conventional. There's a component of something called ketamine, but there's more to it."

Sterling's frown deepened. "Ketamine? That's a bloody date rape drug!"

"Er, yes, sir, I know."

"What would Solly have a date rape drug in his system for? That's something that's used on women!"

Rita couldn't help but observe that his outrage wasn't at the apparent use of such a drug, but that it had been used on a <u>male</u>. She said, "I'm sorry, sir. I've no explanation to offer. Neither has Doctor Cartwright. She's simply made the observation that there's a significant level of this substance in the deceased's body. It's part ketamine, with at least one other substance."

"What substance?"

"She's not entirely sure sir, or at least, is puzzled. It appears to be pure nicotine."

"Solly didn't smoke at all, as far as I know. Took his football too seriously for that."

"I can only tell you what I'm reading, sir. I'll ask the coroner for more information, shall I?" She handed the report over to him. "It <u>is</u> quite thorough, sir."

Sterling scanned the document. As usual, much of the scientific detail washed over him without leaving a mark.

"Mm, well, it doesn't make sense to me. I want to know how something like that gets into the system of a non-smoker."

"I can only ask, sir, but you're right. It does seem highly unusual."

"Highly unusual, and highly bloody suspicious," he replied.

Sterling threw file and photo down onto his desk with feeling.

.ooo.

6

———————

That morning, long before Chris Derbishire's visit, Arthur and Cianawyn had decided to make a change to their regular routine. Instead of coffee, cereal and toast in front of the television, they settled down to enjoy their breakfast while listening to the radio. CRD-FM, to be precise.

Not long before, it would have been Mike Salmon's Morning Special providing the backdrop to their repast, but now it was Gordon Teller whose voice rode the community radio air waves.

"It's funny how broadcasting changes a voice," mused Arthur. "When we catch up over coffee, Gordon talks like a bloke just in from the back paddock. Now listen – he's almost smooth."

Cianawyn nodded. "Certainly, he sounds professional. That's not quite what he sounds like in 'real life', you reckon?"

"Do you want to find out for yourself? Join us for coffee at the Flying Saucer later this morning? If I know Gordon, he'll be happy to share a table with a lovely lady. That should even put him on his best behaviour. I expect he'll be pretty happy anyway, what with this regular work!"

"It's a volunteer station – they don't get paid, do they?" asked Cian, surprised.

"No. But it's not about the money for Gordon. It's an ego thing. He likes the prestige of the job."

That prompted a raised eyebrow. "That's funny, Ay – that sounds like some reports I've heard of missing Mike."

Right then, as if there'd been a psychic link in operation, Teller announced, "I have to ask, does any know whatever happened to Mike? Again."

"Hmm – do you think he sounds sincere in his concern, darling?"

"No more sincere than station management expects of him, my love," answered her husband.

With thoughts of Flying Saucer scones to come, the couple decided against more coffee or toast. They spent some productive but casual time in the garden. Arthur did the actual weeding, while Cianawyn did both weed-spotting, and conveying buckets of removed plants to their big 'green waste' bin.

Her instinct for trouble was telling her that something odd was going on. Maybe there was more going on at CRD-FM than met the eye, or ear. Maybe Gordon had a clue about the missing Mike, whether he knew it or not. Arthur agreed: Gordon didn't really think outside himself very much, so he might be missing something.

Mid-morning, they drove into downtown Dunbar. As they strolled into the coffee shop, a grizzled man wearing a colourful waistcoat over his white shirt and jeans called out.

"Artie! Over here!" he cried, waving. "This beautiful woman must be the darling bride you've told me about! Oh – I hope so, anyway."

"Yes, yes, you got it right, mate. Gordon Teller, meet Cianawyn Lauder."

Although he didn't actually stand up, the announcer did extend his hand to Cianawyn as he bowed his head graciously. She accepted the hand, half expecting the sort of chivalrous kiss on it that her husband sometimes gave. Instead, she received a polite, almost formal handshake.

"Pleased to meet you, Mr. Teller," she said.

"Call me Gordon. Take a seat, both of you. Naomi!" he called, addressing the blonde behind the counter.

Smiling, the woman took their order, and soon delivered their coffees, together with a refill for Gordon, and a plate of fresh warm scones.

"I'm sure Arthur has heard it all before – sorry sweetie – but, what's it like working at the radio station, Gordon?"

The temporary breakfast host waved a casual hand. "It has its moments, good and bad," he said.   .

He was a natural, almost compulsive, raconteur, and launched into a series of stories about events and personalities around the station.

Gordon painted a picture of an organization that was effectively split on gender lines. Most of the 'on-air' people were male, while the administration was an exclusively female domain. Two of the ladies were the only staff actually on a payroll. Gloria Barnet was the very recently-appointed station manager, and Desley Hattersley was the long-standing advertising manager.

"Old Glory seems pretty good," Gordon conceded. "It was her that decided to give me a go on the breakfast shift. Making up her own mind instead of listening to gossip."

"That's always a good approach," agreed Cianawyn, before cautiously asking, "Were you on the wrong end of some gossip?"

"A few times, yeah. I should have had a bigger role in CRD a long time ago, but I'm not as pretty or charming as Mike bloody Salmon. Desley – the Mad Hatter I call her – has been smitten with Mike for years. She got him into the plum shift. But it hasn't helped that a few of the producers have had their noses out of joint with me."

"Oh? Why's that?" asked Arthur, already having heard the details before, but opening the window of opportunity for his wife to learn some more.

"Marietta Columba is peeved that I asked her out a couple of times. Patty Crohn is peeved that I never asked her out. And the young 'un from Uni, Angie, has listened to the rubbish from the pair of them."

This 'Angie', Cianawyn knew, would be the same Angelika Judd that was one of the Dunbar & District Players. Silently, Cianawyn thought that didn't sound quite like the Angelika she was coming to know in *Sweeney Todd*, who seemed a much more independent thinker.

"What annoys me," Gordon continued, "I get in strife for trying to hit onto one or two of the girls now and then, but bloody Salmon tried it on all the time and they were falling over themselves to work with him! He got away with it, I get complained about!"

"And it wasn't because of his looks, you reckon," said Arthur sympathetically, if not entirely sincerely.

Cianawyn played a diplomatic card, too. "Mike did sound pleasant. Not as professional as you, but chatty."

"That's been the CRD style for a while," said Gordon. "I reckon that's part of why I only ever get fill-in jobs. I sound more like I belong on ABC Classical."

Arthur grinned. "You're no more a Groovy Young Thing than I am these days, mate."

That won a laugh from Teller. "The sad thing is, Artie, Mike was our age at least, and all of us are a bloody sight younger than Fitzroy Carlson!"

"Hi, Fitzroy!" called both Cianawyn and Arthur in silly falsetto voices.

That was the regular catchphrase of the man who had held down the 9-till-noon shift at CRD-FM for years, and who also hosted an 'old time rock and roll' program on weekends. During his times on air, a 'glee club' rendition of the cry by a gaggle of children was played with annoying frequency.

"The old bugger would have liked to take over the breakfast slot as well as what he's got now, I reckon," mused Gordon.

"Could he have done that?" asked Cianawyn.

A snort from Gordon made his opinion clear. "No chance. He can barely make it in to the studio in time for a nine o'clock start. You know he's nearly eighty?"

"Really? He doesn't sound it! Not young, obviously, but not *that* old."

"Dear girl, he's been doing the Hip Modern DJ thing for at least fifty years, nearly twenty of them as a volunteer since he got too crotchety for the mainstream stations to employ him. I'll tell you what, you think I don't have much time for Mike Salmon? Old Fitz really resented him. His reputation, public profile, all that. *'I am the face of Community Radio Dunbar!'* he used to tell anyone and everyone."

"Which is ironic, since nobody knows what either of them look like, what with it being radio," said Arthur with a chuckle.

"That's true," Cianawyn said thoughtfully. "I think very few people in the community know what Mike looks like. You hear a voice on the radio, but have no concept of the face behind the voice. Not his, or yours, or Fitzroy Carlson's. Eighty? Wow – he still comes across as bright and breezy."

"Whereas in reality, he looks like he's out on a day pass from a High Dependency Old Folks' Home," replied Gordon, amused at his own wit.

There was some irony in this, in that Gordon was not a young man himself. Despite the cheerful banter between them, Cianawyn was sure the radio announcer was quite a bit older than her darling husband.

More than a little affronted at his tactlessness, Cianawyn said coldly, "You do know that my mother lives in an Assisted Living facility?"

Without so much as a blush, Gordon immediately switched into Charming mode. "That may be so, dear lady, but I'm sure if she's anything like you, if you take after her, she certainly won't <u>look</u> as though she lives in such an environment. Fitzroy on the other hand, looks... well... the man gets around on a wheelie walker."

"As does my mother."

"Yes, but I'm sure she does it with a lot more style than Fitzroy does."

Arthur tried to defuse the sudden tension. "And to be fair, my love, your Mum doesn't have the temerity to hold down a position as the DJ for a rock music show that might be an opportunity for somebody half the age."

It was a fair point, and Cianawyn put a lid back on her irritation. Diplomatically the subject was changed, and for a while she let her beloved carry most of the conversation while she watched and listened.

Gordon Teller, she realized, was almost two characters in one – the witty intelligent charmer, and the bitter misogynistic grump, and the change between the two could be mercurial. Either could be infuriatingly sexist, but she also realized that the man himself was blissfully unaware of that. She thought that he'd probably be shocked by such an accusation. She could imagine the response: 'No! I really *like* women!'.

Eventually the conversation meandered back in the direction of missing Mike Salmon.

"Maybe, when you're broadcasting your 'does anyone know his whereabouts' piece, you could give a description?" suggested Cianawyn. "What *does* he look like?"

Gordon shrugged. "Pretty ordinary, really. A strange bloke sometimes, but he didn't look it. A bit taller than me – about Artie's height. He was probably blonde in his younger days, but more grey now. Clean shaven. Flabby, if not exactly fat. Nothing to make him stand out in a crowd, which is probably why he went in for loud gear. Hawaiian shirts, that sort of thing."

Cianawyn, deep in thought, turned to Arthur. "Does it sound like it could have been him you saw... on the beach, that day?"

Without fully engaging his brain, Bayer responded, "What would a breakfast deejay be doing in the ocean?"

Unaware of the real thread of their conversation, Gordon casually said, "Actually, Mike did do a bit of fishing. Not as keen as his brother, but I know he dipped a line occasionally."

He checked his watch, then leaned forward and said quietly, "If you good folks don't mind, I happen to know that young Naomi goes on her break shortly, and I know she's been very keen to have lunch with me. Would you mind, er..."

"Making ourselves scarce? No worries," replied Arthur softly.

In a similar undertone, Cianawyn concurred, "Okay, we'll just leave you to that, shall we?"

The couple exchanged looks, Arthur gave Gordon a small nod and a wink, and they made a diplomatic exit just as Naomi appeared to be heading for their table, exchanging waves as they passed.

Both had observed that 'young Naomi' wasn't really that young, but it's a relative term. Whether she did, in fact, go on a lunch date with Gordon wasn't something that either the waitress or the announcer subsequently talked about. Each probably had their own reasons for that, which may or may not be significant. But the married pair decided that it was none of their business.

As Arthur parked the station wagon in the garage of their bungalow, Cianawyn was mulling over the earlier conversation. She was firming in her hunch that there was a connection between the missing man and the mysterious disappearing body that her husband had seen. All she was going on was instinct, but she shared with her mother a high regard for intuition, especially her own.

She gave voice to her musing. "So – it wouldn't be implausible for Mike to be out in the ocean."

"Naked?" asked Arthur as he turned off the engine.

"Less common for a fisherman, I admit, but Gordon did say there were stories that he was a bit of a strange cove, didn't he? And I've heard that from other sources, too. Who knows?"

Arthur frowned as he got out of the car. "Hmm, you'd like to think somebody actually knows something, in amongst all the rumour and innuendo."

.ooo.

7

Not for the first time, Rita Mulholland was wishing that Dunbar Police Station had more than two Detective officers on the books.

Sterling had decreed that he would not be conducting interviews in the rugby league club, or with anyone directly associated with the club. He used the explanation (or excuse) that it might be perceived as a conflict of interest, he being a "well recognized and respected member there".

She had to concede that there was some validity to the point, although she may have phrased things differently. Nonetheless, it put her into an environment where she didn't feel at all comfortable. Speaking to people in administrative positions would be one thing. Perhaps the coach may turn out to be okay. But she knew that soon enough, she'd have to speak with individual players.

It wasn't something she was looking forward to. Her limited exposure already had indicated that the Dunbar Demons RLFC had a culture that she feared would prove to be a swamp of toxic masculinity.

She had no problem with masculinity, but this offered a large streak of misogyny, or as her sister would call it, old-fashioned knuckle-dragging ignorance. A woman's place was not in the dressing room of the footy club, or on the field, it was behind the bar or in the canteen. Making scones and coffee, or pouring beers for the hard-working team and officials, those were the best contributions a woman was expected to make, she feared. The enlightenment of women's football had yet to shine upon the Dunbar clubrooms, it seemed, by what she could glean from Bob Sterling.

For the first round of interviews, conducted early on Tuesday afternoon, Rita had only a limited range of options when she'd tried to make appointments. The first-grade coach, Bill Cameron, who was the only actual employee of a Club run on volunteer labour, and even then, wasn't full-time; Alfie Hansell, officially the general handyman and bootboy, a long-retired halfback and builders' labourer who really hung around the Club (and was permitted to do so) because he had no idea of what else to do with his life; and the Chairman of the Demons' Management Board, thus effectively the boss, Trevor Salmon.

As the owner and Managing Director of his own development company, Trevor was able to give himself enough time off to grant the detective a brief interview. Fifteen minutes at the absolute most, he'd warned that morning when she'd called to arrange an appointment.

Reviewing her notes later, Mulholland mused that she could hardly have encountered three more different personalities in one place in one afternoon.

Alfie claimed to not know his own age. That was plausible. He clearly showed the combined effect of age, minimal education, and a long history of head knocks in his playing career. By the look of him, and based on the approximate dates of some of the "bloody huge games" that he claimed to remember playing in, she'd guess him to be in his seventies. He might have been older, or he may have been younger but had a really, really hard life.

What he wasn't, was helpful. Whatever experiences Alfie Hansell had had with women over the years clearly hadn't been good. For a start, he refused to talk with her in the changing room where he'd been working.

"No bloody women allowed in here. No place for 'em," he'd snapped.

The interview, such as it was, happened near the edge of the playing field. Not actually <u>on</u> it, of course. The hallowed surface of Tate Park was no place for a woman either, in Alfie's opinion.

Mulholland's introductory questions about the veteran bootboy's own background unleashed a torrent of information. Much of it was garbled, and possibly spurious, and most of it was useless.

Hansell had been there, he said, since the days when Dunbar was "nothin' but a piddly-squit little bloody fishing village". That seemed unlikely to Rita, since she knew that the town had existed for over a hundred years, and had apparently grown quickly in its early years on the back of a successful commercial fishing industry.

Alfie had joined the Club when he was "a tough little tacker, still in school". That formal education had ended early in his life, which was a good thing as far as he was concerned, learning far more in the School Of Hard Knocks.

There had been the time when the wall of a house he'd been working on had collapsed. A bigger bloke would have been killed, but the falling wall timbers had landed on either side of him, and the joist missed him when he ducked.

"See, I'd learned the importance of keepin' me bloody head down. Same on the footy field. Keep me head down, and let the big bastards go over the bloody top of me. I remember a game I played for the country rep side. This oversized bugger from Redfern or somewhere kept tryin' to bust me in the chops, but I..."

Rambling reminiscences made up much of Hansell's speech (it was mostly too one-sided to be called a dialogue), but Rita did manage to occasionally drag him back to the topic she was interested in. Yes, the old man knew Solomona Tuafeulaki. Sort of.

"One of them big Fijian blokes. Or Tonga or New Guinea or some bloody place. All look the same to me. Oh, don't get me wrong, nice enough bloke. A lot of 'em are. Quiet. Respectful. You get the odd bad one. I remember one bugger, went on to play for Perkins Bay Pirates down the coast. Spent one whole game lookin' for a bloody fight , didn't care if it was with the opposition or one of his own team. Got one in the end, too. I remember our Roger…"

"Ah – Mr. Hansell? About Solomona?"

"Oh yeah, him. Islander of some sort. Game's full of 'em now. Bloody great long names no bugger can pronounce. Never used to see any of 'em. White blokes' game back when I was playin'. Now we're the bloody minority – all these big dark buggers. Solly's one of <u>them</u>. Not a bad fella, I think. Them names confuse me. All of our blokes are alright. Hard, but well-behaved. Young Bill won't have 'em in the Club if the cause trouble. He gave a couple the flick not long back."

"Bill? Bill Cameron, the coach?"

"That's him. Ah, he was a bloody good player a few years back. All the skills. Shoulda gone a lot further in the game, but too nice, I reckon. You need a bit of mongrel in you. That's what got me by. I remember…"

Rita managed to cut him off. "Did Solomona get on with the coach?"

"Bill gets on with all the boys. Hated getting' rid o' them two trouble-makers, even. He gets on with everybody, I reckon. I <u>said</u> he was too nice. Oughta toughen them up a bit. Oh, they're winnin' games alright, but I don't reckon the other sides fear Dunbar any more. They're afraid of losin', but they ain't afraid of getting' hurt, not like they used to be."

Alfie's inability to remember one multi-syllabic name from another was a severe impediment to his value as a witness. The Demons' Polynesian players didn't seem to exist as individuals for him. It was as though they were a collective entity, and one which existed outside the constraints of time. Alfie mentioned a couple who'd played for Dunbar in the 1980s, with no indication that they'd ever retired, which seemed more than unlikely to the detective.

She tried to explore whatever did happen to players who retired or otherwise departed, but it seemed that in Alfie Hansell's world, anyone who left the Club stopped being of interest unless they became an opponent, and anyone who left the great game itself effectively ceased to exist. That would be Solomona Tuafeulaki's fate,

Mulholland realized. Not that he'd occupied any individual space in Alfie's world in the first place.

Rita left Alfie at the door of the groundskeeper's shed, another male-only sanctum, allowing the garrulous old man to get on with some "maintenance work on the bloody mowers and trimmers and such. New bloody gardener lets the blades get blunt."

She walked away with him grumbling about "young people today", and headed back towards the clubhouse. The coach was there, in his downstairs office, waiting for her. After her experience with Alfie Hansell, Rita was reluctant to ask for much of the man's own personal history, but she quickly relaxed.

At first sight, Bill Cameron did not look like a former rugby league player. Not the stereotypical image, anyway. He was tall and well-built, yes, but he had clear and intelligent eyes, and a face that showed no signs of structural damage. He smiled and Rita noted that, yes, even his teeth were almost perfect, with just enough asymmetry to prove that they were real.

Politely he stood and extended a hand as she entered the room. "Detective Mulholland, I presume. Hello – I'm Bill Cameron."

"Good afternoon. Nice to meet you." She was sincere. The man's difference to Alfie was immediately evident, and a relief. "Please, sit down," she said.

"Thanks. Now, I understand you want to talk about one of my players?"

"Yes, that's right. Solomona Tuafeulaki."

"Solly? He's not in trouble, is he? He's one of the last fellows I'd think would go off the rails!"

Bob Sterling, at that moment, may have made an injudicious remark about it not being rails that Solly had gone off. Fortunately, Rita was too diplomatic to indulge in her boss' tactless 'wit'. Gently she explained the circumstances of her visit.

Some of the colour drained from Cameron's smooth, tanned face. "That's... that's awful! Do you know what...? No, I guess not, or you wouldn't be here now."

"Exactly. I appreciate that this may be difficult. It's clear that you care about your players. When did you last see him?"

"At training on Thursday night. Here. Seemed normal enough, although he's been a little down on form over the past few weeks. I gave the boys a fairly light run that night, because the first-grade side had the bye on the weekend."

"So, Solomona didn't play last Saturday?"

"No. I gave them all the weekend off. I did hope that a few of them would turn up to support the reserves in their game. Now I think of it, I <u>was</u> surprised that Solly wasn't among the few who did. He's usually such a good club man. I assumed he must have gone on the fishing trip some of the lads were getting together."

"A fishing trip? Interesting. Know any details?"

"Very few, I'm afraid, sorry. I <u>think</u> the Latukefu brothers were organizing it, but I couldn't even swear to that."

"Okay, I'll be asking some questions about that when I meet with the players this week. You train on Thursday evenings?"

"Yes. Tuesdays as well, if you want to hang around tonight and talk to the boys when we're done?"

"Hmm, if I'm trying to talk to them one-on-one that could be tricky, as well as making for a long day and night..."

"Oh, of course. Look, I can work up a roster, and send them to see you in the bar, one at a time. How long will you need with each of them?"

"Bit of a 'how long is a piece of string' question, I'm afraid, Mr. Cameron."

"Please, call me Bill."

"Okay, Bill. Hopefully about ten minutes. Some will be less, some more, I imagine, if they have something useful to tell me. I don't need talk for talk's sake."

"You've met Alfie, then."

Their shared laughter broke some of the tension of the situation, but Rita forced herself to quickly resume her serious professional manner.

"Let's make it Thursday. After speaking with you, I'm to meet with the Club Chairman for a bit. I suspect I'll have enough to be starting with this evening as it is. Now, I have to ask for whatever personal details you can give me about Solomona."

Cameron sighed and was silent for some moments. His hand tapped his thigh as he assembled his thoughts. "One of the quieter lads. A good trainer. Very good. Keen to better himself, with hopes to play professionally."

"Realistic hopes?"

"Quite possibly. I know he'd spoken with Trevor Salmon about a tryout for one of the Sydney clubs at the end of our season. Our boss has a few contacts – he commutes down there often on business. So, Solly worked hard, and as far as I know, kept his nose clean, as they say."

The detective nodded as she wrote. "That leads me to my next question. What do you know about the young man's private life?"

"Not a great deal, admittedly. He has – had - a job in a pet store in town. Liked animals. I think he hoped to study veterinary science, but I don't think his school results were quite good enough. Had some hopes that Trevor might be able to help him there, too, I gathered. What else...? Solly comes, came, from a religious family, like a lot of the Tongan boys. Although I don't think he was a big church-goer himself, it certainly had a good influence on his character. I know he did leave home earlier this year, settled into a place on his own. I thought that adjustment was contributing to the recent dip in his form. But the move didn't seem to affect his behaviour in any way that I could see. Didn't smoke. Had the odd drink with the boys, but never to excess, from all I've seen and heard."

"A good moral compass, you'd say?"

"Definitely. A combination of his upbringing and his ambition. Not the 'my body is a temple' vanity some of our lads are prone to, he did know how to enjoy himself. But in moderation. Never to the extent of compromising his fitness."

Mulholland consulted an earlier page of her notebook. She kept her expression and voice carefully neutral as she asked, "Would it surprise you to learn that Mr. Tuafeulaki's body was found to have significant evidence of drug use?"

Once more the colour drained from the coach's face. "No. Not surprised. Shocked! Are you sure?"

"Autopsies don't usually lie, Bill, I'm sorry. And we have a very, very good coroner."

"Sorry, no offence intended. But – Solly? There's never been so much as a hint of it. Like I said, he doesn't smoke cigarettes, nothing more than the odd beer after a game... Do you know what sort of – substance?"

"Something unusual."

"Some kind of steroid? Performance enhancing?"

Rita looked Cameron squarely in the eye and asked, "Have you seen any evidence of anything like that?"

The coach looked away, uncertainly rather than guiltily, Mulholland thought. "Um... no. He's been fitter this year, played with more energy, until recently. But I've chalked that up to more training, better commitment, that desire to turn professional. It really hasn't looked like anything more."

"Hmm... As I say, it's a rather unusual substance that was found in his system. It may not have been meant to be performance-enhancing. Not on the football field, at any rate."

"Eh? What do you mean?"

"The body was found at the base of High Point. The place does have a certain reputation. I asked about Solomona's private life. Was he in a relationship? Of any sort?"

Bill Cameron looked thoughtful. "Not that I'm aware of. Nothing that he ever spoke about, far less bragged about, like some of the boys."

"So, it is possible that if he was in a relationship, it was clandestine."

"Possible, I suppose. He may have mentioned something to some of the other lads. I'd <u>like</u> to think that they keep no secrets from me, but I guess it's impossible to be sure."

Once more, Rita nodded. She glanced at her watch and said, "I must go. I've an appointment to talk with your Club President. Can we continue this in twenty minutes or so, please?"

The coach appeared genuinely contrite as he replied, "I'm sorry, no. I do have another appointment that I'm already at risk of being late for."

"Oh, my apologies…"

"No, no. You're doing your job, and it's important. I understand. You'll be back on Thursday evening?"

"Yes. Perhaps I can talk with you before or after I've spoken to the team?"

"After would be better, if you're able to hang around. The clubhouse bar doesn't open after training, but I can offer you a coffee that isn't too horrible."

"It cannot be worse than what we have at the station. Yes, thank you. I can work late, although it's better if I can plan for it. It comes with the job."

"Oh, can I break the news to the boys tonight? Or is that for you to do on Thursday evening?"

"No, it's fine. I'll be surprised if word hadn't gotten out by then anyway, if it hasn't already. No detail, though, please. Just tell them Mr. Tuafeulaki's body has been found."

"I can do that. I'll see you on Thursday."

The two shook hands, and exchanged cautious smiles. The coach departed, and the detective made her way up the concrete stairs to the Members' bar room. She sat at one of the small tables, and wrote in her ever-present notebook.

She found herself thinking that she really did not want Bill Cameron to be involved in this case in any negative way. She pursed her lips. That realization was dangerous. Implied some cloudiness of thinking, or the potential for it. Of course, the coach had to be considered a 'person of interest'. Unfortunately.

Just as she pondered this, her third interviewee of the day walked up the concrete stairs. He strode up to her table, and sat down without introducing himself.

"Mr. Salmon, I presume," the detective said, without rancour.

The man nodded. "Call me Trevor," he replied in a voice similarly neutral.

Rita looked at the newcomer as she turned to a new page in her notebook. A little taller than she was. Hair the colour of an old hay bale. Square jawed with a shadow of stubble. Grey eyes with an intense gaze.

"Now, what's this about?" he asked.

'Straight to the point, just as polite as he has to be, and no more,' was Mulholland's private note to herself.

Aloud, she explained about Solomona Tuafeulaki's death. No more details than necessary, and no suggestions or implications. Just bare facts.

Salmon nodded. "Damn shame. The kid had promise."

"I understand you'd organized a tryout for him with a Sydney club."

"Yeah. Like I said, he had potential."

"So, you knew him pretty well?"

"No. I've watched him play, and I like to think I'm a good judge. I talked to his coach, who speaks highly of his attitude and personality. Beyond that, I don't really know him any better than any of the other players at the club. I'm a keen observer, but I don't want to do any of the coaches' jobs."

"I understand. You don't mix with the players socially?"

"We'll see each other at functions. I try to drop in to post-match celebrations, or commiserations, when I can. But no, we don't mix."

Rita wrote for a few moments. "Outside of the Demons, what do you do, Mr. Salmon?"

"Trevor. Lots. Too much, I sometimes think. I run a development company, SageCorp. Extremely busy at present, establishing a new estate just this side of Shelley Bay."

"I've read about that. Percival Point, isn't it? You're running into a lot of local resistance, I understand."

"You always get that in my business. The Not In My Backyard brigade. The tree huggers who are already in their own comfortable homes. The rent-a-crowd protesters. Minor irritations. The business of clearing and constructing is far more important to me."

"So, the Dunbar Demons are a relief valve for you?"

"When we're winning, yes." Trevor's smile looked genuine. "Good for part of the year, at least. And I do have my dogs."

"Working dogs, or pets?"

"I certainly think of them as working – hope so, anyway. I have a stable of racing greyhounds. They take up a fair bit of my attention. I'm more 'hands on' with them than I am with the footballers."

"I see." More writing. "Is that what led Solomona Tuafeulaki to talk to you about veterinary studies?"

"Eh? Oh – oh yes, that's right. I'd intended to speak to a friend in Sydney about some sort of training, if the move to there worked out."

"It's your work that has you back and forward between here and Sydney?"

"Frequently. Meetings, mostly, usually about money and planning approvals. Sometimes I'll be looking at something to do with the dogs."

"I see. Where do you actually <u>live</u>, Trevor?"

"I keep an apartment in Newtown, and I've got a place up here at the Dunes."

"Wouldn't it be more convenient to live nearer to the new development?"

"Who'd want to live at Percy Point? It's like the rest of Shelley Bay – full of spoilt brats, dropouts and tourists."

Mulholland made a brief note about the attitude of the developer to the people likely to be most affected by his project.

"At the Dunes, you say? The most expensive real estate in Dunbar," she observed.

"It is now, yes. It was my parents' beach house. They're long gone now. It's quite large. I share it with my brother Michael, normally."

"Normally?"

"Oh, he's gone walkabout. I haven't seen him for a couple of weeks."

"Have you lodged a Missing Person report? Does this happen often?" asked the de4tective.

Salmon shrugged. "Not often, not these days. But he's always been a bit flighty. He calls it 'artistic temperament'. I learned a long time ago not to waste my time arguing with him. Is there anything more you want to know about the Fijian lad?"

"I thought Mr. Cameron said he was Tongan."

"Whatever – islander of some sort. I did say I didn't know him particularly well."

"I don't think so. You're not aware of any reports of trouble with him?"

"No."

"Have you any idea of if he was in any sort of relationship?"

Trevor frowned as he thought. "No. When we talked about the possibility of a move to Sydney, he made no mention of having a partner to worry about, if that helps."

"It might, thank you. We'll be talking to his family, of course."

"Hmm – you may not get much help there. Very religious lot. I don't think they approved of playing games on a Sunday, and when they found out he'd rather be a footballer than a missionary, they cut off most contact."

"Interesting, thanks," said Mulholland. 'And somewhat different to Bill Cameron's observations,' she thought.

"Fine," said Salmon. "If you need me again, just call my office and make an appointment. Happy to help however I can."

"Thank you," Rita said, shaking the proffered hand.

The Club President left the room in long, confident strides. Rita tapped her pen on the open notebook. Certainly, he hadn't been unhelpful or evasive. Not about Solomona Tuafeulaki, at any rate. There was something that she felt was not quite right about Trevor's absent brother. Then again, she knew she was close to her own two sisters, so perhaps such a different sibling relationship just seemed alien to her. It wasn't relevant to the case in hand, anyway.

There would be little to report to D. S. Sterling. She hoped that he'd learned more from talking with the Tuafeulaki family. At least, there might be some resolution of the different impressions she'd gotten from the coach and the boss.

None of the interviews had added much to her understanding of the victim. She found herself taking some comfort from the prospect of talking again with one of the three men, at least.

.ooo.

8

Detective Sergeant Sterling was twirling his pen in his fingers in the manner that he did when he was <u>particularly</u> irritated with the world.

Clearly, the interview with Solomona's family had not gone very well. He'd never admit it, but he knew he needed Rita Mulholland's help with this one. Sterling was the senior officer, but the reality was that she was the thinker of the pair.

The Detective Sergeant had risen above his level of competence by a combination of bull-headedness and circumstance. When the vacancy had arisen, there had been no-one more able who'd been willing to move to Dunbar, and nobody more able already available within the station.

Since then, he'd held the job competently, but with minimal challenges. That had thwarted his ambitions, as far as he was concerned. He'd wanted that One Big Case to attract the admiring attention of senior officers in the south. There <u>had</u> been a multiple murder case recently, but somehow, he didn't feel that he'd received adequate recognition for the way it had been resolved.

Now there was another suspicious death, but he knew he had to tread carefully. If his seniors discovered he was close to the dead man's football club, and the Club turned out to be somehow relevant to the man's suicide (he was still sure that's what it was), that could lead to awkward questions. Sterling hated awkward questions when it wasn't him asking them.

After a discreet knock on the door, Rita entered his office. His mood was obvious, nevertheless Rita asked her question. She needed all the information that she could gather.

"How did the interview with the Tuafeulaki family go, sir?" she asked quietly, preparing herself for a sharp response.

She wasn't disappointed.

"Hmph. Bloody Jehovah's Witnesses or some such. Something worse, I think. <u>Extremely</u> bloody religious, anyway. More concerned with the son's soul than his actual death."

"Nothing useful about his private life?"

"Not recently. Young bloke left home about six months ago, moved into a unit on his own, much to their outrage. They'd planned – expected – him to become a missionary for their church. Go off to the wilds of New Guinea or somewhere. The boy wanted to pursue a career as a footballer first. Maybe go Bible-bashing later in life, but that wasn't good enough for them."

"Mm. That tallies with something that the coach told me."

"Yeah, Bill would know. Solly's side of it, at least. Apparently when the kid 'chose to follow the path of wickedness' – that is, moved out to live on his own, they just broke off all communication."

"And that worked both ways?"

"Eventually. Seems the boy tried calling to talk, but until he not only apologised, but renounced the ways of Satan – i.e. quit football, they'd just hang up on him."

"Harsh," said Rita sadly. "I thought there was a great tradition of sport in the islands."

"There is. But there's a big tradition of religion, too. Some very active missionaries building churches up there in the old days."

"But the islands' own culture is older."

Sterling grunted. History wasn't his long suit, but he'd had islander friends in his playing days, and early days on the force.

"Yeah, but the church was more aggro. Pushier, at least. And footy didn't get there until even more recently. Prior to his departure, they reckon he was a good kid. They laid it on a bit thick, in fact, about him being a good Christian boy. Studied hard, respected his parents, went to church. All up until the fiends at the footy club led him astray. Made him a play-er, not a pray-er."

"Fiends? Really?"

"Ah, not quite. But that was the sentiment. Let's say, they don't reckon the Demons' name is a coincidence. Anyway, they reckon they can't tell me anything about what Solomona's been up to for the last six months or so."

"No clues on friends, or relationships?" Mulholland asked, without much optimism.

"No clues, and no interest, I reckon. Anyone who isn't part of their congregation just doesn't seem to matter to them, family or not," muttered the Detective Sergeant.

"I see." Again, that sort of family dynamic was quiet alien to the young woman.

The pair sat in thoughtful silence for a while, until Mulholland looked up from her notes and asked, "Sir? I wonder if, given what we now know about the drugs found in Mr. Tuafeulaki's system, we should go over his flat again in more detail? I know you and a constable had a quick look, hoping for something like a suicide note, but now...?"

Still fiddling with the pen, Sterling replied, "Yeah, you're probably right. Take one of the uniforms with you, and take care of it tomorrow. I'll take another couple of them with me, and we'll go over that area up top of High Point with a fine-tooth comb. I know we taped some of it off, but a snogging spot like that, who knows if anyone paid any attention to a bit of yellow plastic, eh? Still, can only try."

Dismissed, Rita went back to her own desk. Her boss now seemed to be approaching this case with more consideration than usual. He <u>must</u> be rattled by it, she thought.

.ooo.

9

—————

Tuesday evening was rehearsal time. Backstage at the Terrence Community Theatre, Cianawyn sat in a plastic chair watching Angelika Judd turn a slow pirouette. The costume mistress nodded approvingly.

"The fit's good. Thanks, Angelika. I'll take it home and replace the tacking with stitches that'll hold up to your being chased across the stage."

"Thanks! I'd hate to have it fall apart under the spotlights! Although, there might have been some who'd enjoy that..." the young woman replied.

Cianawyn looked puzzled, so the actress explained. "You never met Mike, did you? Sorry. Having to put up with him at the radio station as well probably doesn't help. I volunteer there as a producer a couple of times per week. He could be a bit of a sleaze. Well, I thought so. Other girls who've worked with him, on this show and before, reckon he's harmless. But I often found Mike... a little creepy."

Miracle had just walked in and caught the tail end of the conversation.

"Really?" she said. "I thought he was nice. He always seemed interested in me. He mentioned wanting to help my acting career, but nothing came of it before he went away."

Angelika gave a short laugh as she extricated herself from the Victorian-style dress. "He said something similar to me, once. I suppose he might have been sincere. Ask some of the girls who've been with the Players longer."

All of this was being filed away in Cianawyn's memory, but she said nothing about it. Instead, she asked Miracle to try on the jacket that she'd made for her.

"Hmm," the dressmaker murmured, thoughtfully. "A bit snug. You're still too obviously female."

"Umm... I can't help that, sorry."

Cianawyn smiled. "I know, Miracle. I'll let the jacket out, make it a bit looser. Maybe we can find you a bandeau top to wear under your shirt."

"A what?"

"Kind of a strapless bra. Elasticised cotton. I'll try to get one a size too small, to – er – flatten you out a bit. It might be a bit uncomfortable, but it's not a long show so you won't have to put up with it for too long."

"I don't mind. I'll do whatever I have to do to be a performer."

"Good, thanks," said Cianawyn, silently wondering if that might be a dangerous attitude for a young woman to have. "It shouldn't affect your singing, but we'll try it out as soon as possible to check."

"Okay," said the girl happily, slipping back into the colourful t-shirt she'd been wearing.

Both girls went out to join the warm-up breathing exercises that Shauna now started rehearsals with.

Young Han Soo Thie came and went for his fitting in short order. His ragged costume was simple, and would require little adjustment. All that Cianawyn learned in her brief chat was that, the name of their restaurant notwithstanding, Han's family were Malaysian Chinese, not Thai.

"How many people here know the difference?" the young man had asked, without rancour, before rejoining the warm-up on stage.

That allowed Cianawyn a couple of minutes to ponder upon some of the remarks she'd heard, particularly those of the two girls.

Her reflections were interrupted by a knock on the dressing room door.

"Come in. Oh, hi Alan," she said.

"Evening, Ms. Shanwin."

It was as close as most people came to pronouncing her name correctly. Getting it right first time had been one of the things that had endeared Arthur Bayer to her immediately. But he was in the minority, and she'd learned to be forgiving.

The women's dressing room happened to be more than twice the size of that reserved for the males, so Cianawyn had chosen to do all of her fittings there.

"Good evening, Alan. You're okay with missing the warm-up?"

The recently-recast Sweeney Todd laughed quietly. "Ha – I keep telling Shauna, I know how to breathe! Your husband tells her the same thing, and that he's had even more years of practice at it than me. But she does insist, unless we have a good excuse, such as consulting with our lovely costume lady!"

Alan Strong's gentle flattery brought a smile to her face. "Very good. I'll expect to see Arthur straight after you, then."

"Er, maybe not. I think Shauna figures you'll be fitting him up at home."

"Oh dear, that's his escape plan blown, then. Now, try this cloak on please, and the pants. I'm still working on what sort of top you should have."

"Black and sinister is all I've been told."

"Yes, likewise. Not a lot of help to me, I'm afraid. I'll identify some type of period shirt I suppose. And a black apron – you <u>are</u> a barber, after all."

"What about some blood stains on the apron? Discreet or otherwise?" he suggested.

"What an excellent idea! Not blood-soaked, but enough to catch the more alert eyes in the audience. Good man!"

"Oh, this cape is great!" exclaimed the actor, giving it as dramatic a swirl as he could within the confines of the dressing room. "Being the bad guy is so much more fun than playing the straight man, like Colonel Jeffrey. No offence to your husband intended!"

"None taken, by me at least. So, I imagine you're quite glad of Mike's abrupt departure."

"Oh, yes!" He posed in front of a mirror, trying out a few melodramatic menacing expressions. "For a few reasons, if I'm honest."

"Really?"

The new leading man sat down and lowered his voice. "Yeah. Landing this role, obviously. Mike and I didn't get on very well. Too different natures that just couldn't seem to rub along together. I always found him too quick to criticize, and nastily, not constructively. And, well, frankly, I didn't trust him."

"Oh? Why's that?"

Alan looked around cautiously. "I'm being careful, 'cause he still has friends and supporters here, and I don't want it to sound like sour grapes. But..."

"But?" Cianawyn coaxed, intrigued.

"Well, you know that, outside the theatre, I work at one of the local High Schools?"

"I didn't. Teacher?"

"Used to teach history. Now I'm on the staff of the library. Less stress as I'm getting older."

Looking carefully, Cianawyn judged Alan to be in his mid-fifties, which was only slightly older than correct.

"Anyway," he continued, "I get on well with a lot of the kids, especially since I stopped being a classroom teacher. They talk. To me, and around me, pretty comfortably, and I <u>hear</u> stuff. I mostly let it go in one ear and out the other. Kids are shocking gossips, you know, and not just the girls! But sometimes, when the old alarm bells go off, some stuff sticks."

Her intrigue growing, the seamstress nodded for him to continue.

He went on. "I've heard Mike's name mentioned a few times, not just recently."

"Inappropriate behaviour?" hazarded the wardrobe mistress.

"Not as such, I guess. Not in detail, anyway. Flattery, certainly – from him, I mean, not the kids. And a suggestion that he could 'open certain doors' for the right person. Boy or girl."

"Wow!"

"Given his 'position in the media', or words to that effect," Alan explained.

"You're joking! He's a breakfast announcer on a pokey little community radio station, in, let's face it, a pokey little town!"

"Ah, you and I know that, but to youngsters who've never been more than a half-hour's drive away from Dunbar, he's a media personality. To the more worldly ones, it – he – is a bit of a joke. But for others, I think there's at least some curiosity. And especially when he claims to know 'important people down south', well, it might turn impressionable heads."

Kneeling on the floor to pin the hems of Alan's trousers, Cianawyn looked up, frowning. "Have you told anyone about this? Besides me?"

"No. What's to tell? Some unsubstantiated gossip? Chinese whispers? And Mike is a respected, popular figure in this town. All I've really got is a bit of a bad feeling. I probably shouldn't even have told you, but, with him disappearing like he has, well... I guess I wanted to talk to someone about him. Sorry."

"Don't be. I appreciate the trust. Don't worry, it won't go any further than me." 'And Arthur,' she thought silently. "For what it's worth, I think you're right to be at least a bit concerned. Your duty of care."

"Hah! Yes, I think I'm a lot more concerned than the kids themselves."

"Probably care more in most cases, too."

"Sadly, yes. Thanks for listening."

"That's okay, Alan. Right, I'm done. You can shed the costume bits and go back out now."

"Thanks. With luck, the warm-up is done and I can get on with the real work of rehearsing my arch-villainy!"

"Fingers crossed for you."

Cianawyn looked at the partially finished costumes hanging on a rack beside her. "Depending on who's available, could you send in Dolly, Will or Guy, please?"

Will Marlow and Guy Wilmott were playing the rascally reverend and the romantic male lead, respectively.

Alan nodded. "Dolly will be entrenched behind the piano, I'll bet. I'll see if Will is singing already. If he is, I'll tell Guy to come in."

"Thanks. And thank you for - the chat. I appreciate the trust."

As the actor left, Cianawyn reflected, not for the first time, on what it was that prompted people to launch, unbidden, into deep and meaningful talks with (or, more frequently, _at_) her. Something she'd inherited from her mother. She also reflected on why she suddenly felt so intrigued by Mike Salmon. Instinct, presumably, but nothing she could put into words. Not yet.

Fortunately for the full slate of points to ponder already occupying her head, neither Will nor Guy wanted to discuss anything more than the comfort, or in Guy's case discomfort, of their costumes.

Cianawyn had already established that Guy was something of a whinger anyway. ("That tape measure's cold!" "How long do I have to stand here?" "This material is scratchy!") But in the name of doing a good job, she noted his complaints and figured out ways to address the legitimate ones without adding too much to her workload.

Some time later, she was being driven home by Arthur, with Dolly in the back seat. Fiscal common sense now had them carpooling to and from Golden Gardens whenever possible.

Trying to sound casual, Cianawyn asked the musical director, "What were your impressions of Mike?"

"Charming, when he wanted to be, ducks. A bit full of himself, but. Being honest, I'm surprised he went AWOL on us. He's never got a _lead_ role with the Players before, and he was more than a bit pleased. Not quite being snooty, but... preening, you understand?"

"Was he always like that?" asked Arthur, automatically taking a dislike to a man he'd never met.

"He knew he was a celebrity, put it that way, luvvy."

"Celebrity?" scoffed the driver. "He's the breakfast DJ for CRD-FM for goodness' sake!"

"Around here, that's about as close to a celebrity we get, ducks."

"Relatively big fish in a small pond," observed Cianawyn.

"That's it," agreed Dolly.

"No suggestion of anything... inappropriate?" ventured Cianawyn.

"No-o-o-o," replied Dolly replied, cautiously. "He's always preferred to hang around with the young 'uns, not just in this show. But that's not unusual – by and large, they do tend to be more fun. I 'ave noticed one or two keeping their distance, sideways looks, that sort of thing. But nobody's actually <u>said</u> anything out of order. Not that I've heard."

They travelled in silence for a little while, Arthur concentrating on the road. Cianawyn was remembering days of her youth, one of her first jobs, working for a big motorcycle retailer in Sydney. It took a special sort of confidence for a young woman to call out any sort of abuse, subtle or otherwise, from someone in a position of power. Perceived power, even if that was only bluff.

As if she'd been reading her thoughts, or perhaps pondering memories of her own, Dolly suddenly added, "I'm not just talking about the girls, neither. There's been a couple of lads what I've noticed keeping their distance. Mind you, I have to say, there's at least as many boys and girls what reckon that Mike's a great mate."

Arthur nodded as the security gate of the Estate slid open. "That makes sense," he said. "What did P. T. Barnum say about there being one born every minute?"

"Ooh, that's a bit cynical, luvvy," said Dolly with a smile , as the wagon drew up outside her bungalow. "See you on Thursday," she said with a wave as she got out of the vehicle.

Waving back, Cianawyn found herself thinking of another quote: the worst thing about being a cynic is knowing that you're usually right.

.ooo.

10

The search of Solomona Tuafeulaki's simple one-bedroom flat revealed a few things to the two detectives.

One was that for a young, single, footballer, he was uncharacteristically neat and tidy. Dishes were washed and stacked. Dirty clothes all in a basket ready for the laundry – none scattered on the floor (which, Sterling admitted to himself, would have been what they'd have found in his own bedroom).

Another was that Solomona's alcohol consumption, at home at least, was no more than moderate. There were two cans left of a six-pack of low alcohol beer in the fridge, and no evidence of anything stronger in the flat. Nor were there incriminating cartons, cans or bottles amongst the rubbish. Checking the bins was, of course, a job for Mulholland.

The fact that his wallet still lay untouched on a bedside table suggested that, whatever Tuafeulaki's reason for going to High Point, he hadn't expected to spend any money there (or else was a forgetful young man). All that had been found on his corpse were the keys to his flat and his car. The shiny red sedan had been found in the lookout car park.

The one anomalous thing that they discovered was found in a

small waste bin in the bathroom. It was missed in the initial quick search because it had chanced to fall inside a box that once held a bottle of insect repellent.

'It' was a small, dark brown plastic jar with a screw cap. There was no label, but the faint trace of powder caught in the edge of the bottom of the jar indicated something medicinal, probably tablets. An actual powder would likely have left more residue, the detectives reasoned. The jar was bagged, and would be going to the lab.

The absence of a label was the most suspicious thing about it. Legal drugs always carried some identification, whether they were prescribed or off-the-shelf. There wasn't even a trace of gum on this jar to suggest that a label had been removed.

The other significant thing was actually an absence. There was no sign of a phone. There was an empty plug where a landline was presumably kept by a previous tenant, but no sign of a mobile. There hadn't been one found on the body, either. Nor was there one in the car, which had also been thoroughly searched after it was towed to the yard behind Dunbar Police Station.

Sterling folded his arms and grimaced. "Could he have lost it somewhere?"

"Is it possible he didn't <u>own</u> a phone?" suggested Mulholland.

"He'd be the only bloke his age in the country who didn't. Only <u>person</u>, probably. You'll be at football practice tomorrow night. Ask around. See if anyone has his number."

"Yes, sir. We can check with the different service providers, too. See if he has an account with any of them."

The detective sergeant looked around the lounge room of the small flat. "I reckon we're done here," he said, and moved to the door.

Rita's gaze also swept the room. Could there be anything they'd missed?

The only crockery and glassware not in its cupboard was on the dish drainer beside the sink, so stray fingerprints weren't likely there. Surfaces like tables and sinks were dusted for prints, but didn't seem promising.

No stray tell-tale hairs that obviously didn't match Solomona's were to be seen on floors or pillow.

If he'd had visitors lately, either they were as neat as their host, or they'd been cleaned up after.

In many ways, Solomona Tuafeulaki's life was proving as mysterious as his death.

.ooo.

11

Thursday evening was rehearsal time. And it was a difficult one for the ensemble of *Sweeney Todd*. Director Shauna had succumbed to a throat infection that was starting to go around, as had Dolly and a few of the lead players.

The reins had been passed to the stage manager, Adeline Bond, and that was where the difficulties started. Adeline was very good with all of the technical elements of a stage production, but gave the impression that she thought all shows would be better if not cluttered by actors getting in the way.

Working off the instructions that had been croaked down the phone by Shauna, this rehearsal was to focus on scenes featuring the 'smaller' characters. The director <u>had</u>, more than once, stressed that "there are no small roles, only small actors" but Adeline, with no performing experience of her own, didn't quite grasp that concept. Actors only cluttered her beautifully-designed stage anyway, and anyone other than the leads didn't seem worth the bother.

Still, it was a good opportunity for Cianawyn to check the costumes she'd run up for some of those characters.

The most 'minor' of the players were three playing multiple nameless roles – bystanders, warders and such. All were in their late teens, with more enthusiasm than experience, but plenty of willing-ness to 'pitch in' and help with whatever was required. Brother and sister Nick and Zoe Rankin were in their last year of school, and had been recruited by the two teachers in the cast – Alan Strong and Tom Beaumaris.

With them was a genial young man named Nathan Finnegan. A year older than his two friends, Nathan had no theatrical ambition but was keen to spend time with the undeniably pretty Zoe.

All three had multiple costumes to try on, so Cianawyn had ample time to pursue what had become something of a habit – discreet questioning about the absent Mike Salmon. The 'curiosity gene' she'd inherited from her mother had definitely been activated by the radio announcer's disappearance. Even though it seemed that, officially at least, nobody else was particularly concerned.

The Rankin siblings offered little. They'd had almost no interac-tion with Mike. That surprised Cianawyn somewhat, given the rumblings she'd heard about the man. Both Zoe and Nick were attractive. Perhaps they were too young, she mused. Or perhaps he hadn't known them long enough yet to spin the line of patter she'd heard about.

So, it was surprising then when Nathan casually remarked that he knew Mike "pretty well". It did turn out that the young man was stretching the truth somewhat. It was really his best mate, Ted, who had the connection. And that connection was more with Mike's brother Trev.

Cianawyn was intrigued. She knew nothing of Mike's brother, although, as Nathan's story unfolded she realised that she had heard of his business. Young Finnegan was training as a landscaper. That was a bit of a surprise to the wardrobe mistress – he seemed too slight of build to be lugging decorative boulders and digging out terrace gardens. He explained, though, that his ambition lay in design, not labouring. His mate Ted was the muscle man, and was already working as a fetcher and carrier for Trev Salmon. And it was through Ted that Nathan was looking to secure a job with SageCorp, designing gardens for the new development. It should be at that stage by the time he finished his studies – he'd already spoken with Mr. Salmon about it, he explained confidently.

"With all these connections, it's a wonder young Ted isn't involved with *Sweeney Todd*," remarked Cianawyn with a smile.

"Aw, no. Ted's a good bloke, but he's not the type to be learnin' lines or stage directions. I wanted him to join the stage crew, but, between you and me, he doesn't like Adeline Bond. And I don't reckon he wanted to spend that much time with his Dad, either," said Nathan, discreetly loyal.

"His Dad?" asked Cianawyn, mystified.

"Tom. The madhouse keeper."

The wardrobe mistress looked puzzled, then realised the young man was referring to one of the characters in the play, not Tom's real occupation.

"Ah, Tom Beaumaris," she said, as the penny dropped.

"Yeah. Teaches science at the High School."

Cianawyn nodded her understanding, and, once satisfied that Nathan was comfortable in his warder's uniform, asked the young man to please send Tom in for his fitting.

Tom Beaumaris was a solidly built man in his mid-40s. He'd been a champion rower in his own schooldays, and still had impressively broad shoulders. His character, Jarvis Fogg, was meant to be a disreputable, unattractive figure, so Cianawyn had crafted for him an oversized, almost misshapen coat that emphasised his size but not his musculature.

As she tweaked and trimmed and pinned, the seamstress chatted casually with the teacher. Underwhelmed by the stage manager's approach to rehearsal, he was glad to extend his time in wardrobe as much as possible.

He revealed that he and Alan Strong had worked together for several years, and quickly become friends. It had been that friendship that had drawn him into amateur dramatics, to the delight of his wife Laura who wanted him to express his creativity more.

Ted was their only child. Not the brightest kid, Tom admitted, but he meant well. Cliched as that sounded, the proud father was genuine. His son was a hard worker, determined to do well in his job. Earlier that week, Ted had been rewarded for his efforts at SageCorp by being offered an apprenticeship as a carpenter with the firm's construction team.

The whole family was excited by the opportunity, of course. Obvious parental pride. Tom confided that he and Laura were going to congratulate Ted by buying him his first car. Second hand, of course. A teacher's salary wasn't that good, unfortunately. Cianawyn and Arthur had, in their own opinion, had dodged the bullet of parenthood in theirs and previous relationships, but she could appreciate Tom's paternal pride.

The proud father was grateful for Mike's help in recommending that his brother give Ted a job, although he did admit he didn't particularly like either brother.

"Couldn't say why, really. Funny, isn't it? I'm grateful to both of them, but – you know? Sometimes you just don't take to certain people?"

Cianawyn nodded. She hadn't met either brother, but instinctively thought she'd entirely agree with Tom Beaumaris. After a few snips of loose threads, she was satisfied. With the costume, at least. She frowned at herself. The niggle at the back of her mind was becoming annoying. With a smile, she sent Tom back to rehearsal. He went, with some reluctance, but there honestly was no more to be done with his costumes that evening.

Last to arrive for a fitting were Neil and Mary Fletcher, in the small roles of Judge Brandon and Mrs. Poorlean. Both costumes were quite simple for Cianawyn, and there was little opportunity for much conversation. She already knew that the Fletchers scratched out a living operating a small hardware store, just barely competing with the monolithic chain stores. Their saving grace was that the nearest such competition was in Shelley Bay, just far enough away to deter the lazy or impatient shoppers.

They did mention, though, that they'd originally only become involved with the Dunbar District Players to support their teenaged daughter Georgie.

"She's not in this show, though?" Cianawyn asked, in some surprise.

"Oh, no. She moved to Sydney when she turned sixteen," explained Mary.

"We weren't best pleased, of course," said Neil. "But she'd been convinced that she could really make a career for herself as an actress there, and we didn't want to stand in the way of her ambition."

"Before she left, we were assured that there were people there who'd look after her. I'm afraid we've rather lost contact in the last little while. The odd card on special occasions," added Mary, a little sadly. "We've stayed involved because people here have been so welcoming and supportive, and it's a good distraction for us."

Cianawyn nodded sympathetically, but voiced the question she suspected she already knew the answer to. "Convinced and assured by who?" she asked in her most innocent voice.

"Mike Salmon," was the expected answer from Neil.

"Such a nice man," added Mary. "And his brother Trevor. He was making some of the arrangements."

This was a surprise. Cianawyn hoped that didn't show. She made final adjustments to the judicial robe and the shabby skirt, then waved the Fletchers back to rehearsal – polite and cheerful, but deep in thought.

The seamstress sat quietly in the dressing room. She was listening to the lines being practised, but her mind was elsewhere. What was this obsession with Mike Salmon? She'd heard his voice a few times, but never knowingly seen the man. She trusted her instincts. And her instincts were telling her that this particular absent performer meant trouble.

.ooo.

12

─────────

Thursday evening was time for football practice at Tate Park. And that meant it was time for Rita Mulholland to undertake the task she'd not been looking forward to: interviewing the Dunbar Demons first-team players.

The job proved no more pleasant than she'd expected. Oh, some of the young men were polite. A few were helpful, deliberately or otherwise. Some seemed capable of talking in a vacuum, but keeping them to the point of the interview was challenging. She wondered if they'd taken lessons from Alfie Hansell. Extracting information from others was like drawing blood from a stone.

She did her best to keep things simple for each of them. How well did they know Solomona? Did they spend time with him outside the football club? What were his likes and dislikes? Had they noticed anything different about him recently?

As was her habit, she recorded her observations of each interview in her trusty notebook. At the end of the exercise, though, when reviewing the notes, only five names were asterisked as providing potentially worth following up on.

* <u>Phil Duff</u>. *I'm afraid this young man may be fated to grow into Mr. Hansell. He has many grievances about many things, most of which he*

blamed on the "feral gummint". (I did eventually work out what he was referring to.)

Like others in the team, he works as a builder's labourer for Trevor Salmon's company. In Duff's case, I think his employment is very part-time, when labour is in short supply. He seems averse to the hard work I associate with the building industry.

Duff claims not to have been close to Mr. Tuafeulaki, who he described as "a bit of a goody-goody". By this, I finally determined that the deceased was not inclined towards the drinking and partying that Duff regards as proper behaviour for a footballer after or between games.

Duff asserts that "pretty much" all he and the deceased conversed about was football.

The main value of Duff's interview is the indication that if there was anything in Tuafeulaki's private life which may lead him to suicide, it was not obvious to those around him.

** Daniel Latukefu. Team captain. One of two brothers, of Tongan origin. Daniel is an amiable young man, currently studying veterinary science. Their common interest created some bond of friendship between them, with Latukefu encouraging Solomona to pursue formal training.*

He claims both he and the deceased were actively trying to build a relationship with Trevor Salmon. Daniel was hoping to further his veterinary career with Mr. Salmon's racing interests, but thus far without success. He expressed surprise that Salmon had shown any support for that aspect of Solomona's ambitions, and theorised it was part of the boss' strategy to gain the loyalty of a potential money-earner.

According to Daniel, Solomona's interactions with Mr. Salmon were all about advancing his football career, as well as having some involvement with the racing dogs with an eye to the future. This is consistent with Salmon's own comments. Daniel's observations suggest there may have been more to the relationship between the deceased and Trevor Salmon than the latter indicated. Worth further investigation.

Daniel confirmed that Solomona did have a mobile phone, and was able to give me the number, noted above.

** Jonah Latukefu. Much less co-operative than his brother. Also a University student, in this case, Law. As determined as he was to be conde-*

scending, showing off his legal training and cleverness, there seemed to be some agitation in his manner. Not nervous, but edgy.

Jonah was unable (or unwilling) to provide as much useful information about Solomona as his brother, but his own demeanour makes me suspicious that he knows more than he said.

** <u>Ronny Lofton</u>. Both he and his twin brother Jon are employed by T. Salmon, variously as labourers and dog handlers. Jon Lofton has no other direct connection with the football club, according to his brother.*

Ron described his brother as "too much of a lightweight to be a decent footballer". However, he did make a passing mention of "We're going to do something about that" – a remark he immediately seemed to regret and did not further explain except in the vaguest terms.

I think Lofton is only marginally brighter than Phil Duff, but is at least more ambitious and motivated.

He spoke admiringly of Solomona as a footballer, but said that the deceased had "slipped a bit lately". Again, he made fleeting mention of "doing something about that", and again immediately pulled back, going so far as to deny that he'd said any such thing.

Lofton also said that he and his brother had "quite a bit" to do with Solomona T. while working with the dogs. Again, this seems to contradict some of T. P.'s own statement, although Lofton did not say that Salmon himself was necessarily present at those times.

** <u>Tiki Ravolama</u>. I found it difficult to communicate at all with this young man. His speech was mostly monosyllabic. He never refused to answer a direct question, but his answers were minimal. Did he know the deceased? Yes. How well? Not much. Socially? No. How was he as a team-mate? Good. As a player? Real good. I've heard his form had slipped lately. Had you noticed? I guess. Do you know why? No. Would that mean more opportunity for you? Suppose so.*

I also note that Tiki is another who works for Trevor Salmon, mostly as a labourer. I asked if he worked with the dogs but he shook his head.

The main reason I've noted Tiki as being of interest is his physical condition. Undoubtedly a very fit, strong man, he was sweating (more than might be attributed to coming to the interview from training, compared to the other players), and I noticed a small twitch in the muscles of one arm.

His eyes were restless, unable to hold my gaze, and the pupils seemed small – although this <u>may</u> be a normal condition for him, it seems unlikely. It may have nothing at all to do with Tuafeulaki's death, but I have a sense of something not right.

Rita sat in her car, tapping her pen on the dashboard as she reread her notes. What had she really learned? Not much that was certain. The dead man's phone number. Everything else was hearsay, although some stories corroborated each other.

What there was, was enough to give her cause to suspect there was more to Trevor Salmon than he'd indicated. He didn't necessarily seem to have lied to her, but it appeared that he had more involvement in the lives of the Demons players than he'd let on.

Had Coach Bill Cameron been similarly casual with the truth? Rita found herself sincerely hoping not. She'd see him soon, and it was a meeting that she'd been looking forward to.

.ooo.

13

———

To Rita's relief, football training was soon over. She watched players leave the car park, singly or in groups, in their various vehicles. None appeared to notice her parked a little way along the street. That was entirely as she'd hoped.

Very soon, her mobile phone buzzed. Bill Cameron's name appeared on the screen.

"Hello, Bill," she said, more casually than she felt.

"Hi, Detective Mulholland! The boys have all gone, I've had a quick shower – I'm ready to see you whenever you can make it back here."

"I can be there in two minutes," she replied. "And please, it's Rita. I'm hoping we can just have a nice, friendly conversation. No business."

Unseen, Cameron smiled. He'd been hoping for something like that, but hadn't really expected it. "As you wish - Rita," he replied.

They met outside the Clubhouse, and agreed that there must be more salubrious surroundings for them to enjoy.

On a Thursday night in Dunbar, the options were limited. A few restaurants or pubs, which didn't appeal. But Rita knew of a little wine bar that had opened recently on a side street, a block away from the police station.

"I hope it's still open," she said. "It's a brave business to try in this town, I'm afraid."

The coach smiled. "You're not wrong. But let's reward their optimism."

They were pleased to find that the bar – 'Tristan's' by name, was indeed still open. Two other customers were there, engrossed in their own quiet conversation.

Rita and Bill chose a table on the other side of the room, not that this was very far away. Tristan's was a small venue. A dozen people would have made the interior feel crowded. There were three more tables outside, but their candles were drawing moths and other insects. Better to be inside, admiring the wall art – mostly framed collections of wine labels and champagne crowns. The lighting was low enough to be atmospheric without being gloomy or overtly suggestive.

With two glasses of elegant Loire Valley Sancerre ordered and promptly delivered, the pair started to relax. Both were still conscious that things should be kept on a professional level, but the impulsive decision to make it a more sociable meeting, helped by the excellent white wine, already signalled a level of comfort between them.

Fairly soon, though, Bill felt the need to clear some air. "I know we said 'no business', but look, this is only going to niggle at the back of my mind, and spoil what's shaping up to be a good night out. How did you go with the boys earlier? Anything that could help about Solomona?"

Rita sighed.

"Sorry!" said Cameron hurriedly. I guess it's something you can't talk to me about anyway. Sorry…"

"No! It's alright – don't apologize. You – care about the young men in your team, don't you? I understand."

"It's my job," the coach replied with a shrug.

The detective shook her head. "No. Training them is your job. Caring about them, trying to look out for them, I think that's something you choose to do yourself." She looked into his eyes for a long moment. "Bill, I have to say, officially you're a Person of Interest, so…"

"Is that the same as a suspect?"

He'd hoped for a light laugh, but didn't get it.

"No. Close, but not the same. For one thing, we're not sure that there's been a crime. Solomona's death could have been suicide, or even a terrible accident." Rita paused, still staring at his face. "I trust you. So - I'll talk about this with you, not that there's really a lot to tell. D. S. Sterling won't be pleased if he finds out, mind you."

"Bob? Oh, of course he'd be part of the investigation. Well, I promise I won't tell him anything other than that I've been interviewed by you. Very thoroughly," he said, raising his wine glass.

A smile returned to Rita's face. Carefully she explained some of what she'd heard from the players, implying nor insinuating nothing about any of them.

Coach Cameron nodded thoughtfully. "I'm sorry you didn't get more help from them. Especially sorry about the rude ones. I'm interested in your observations about Tiki Ravolama. He's never been exactly – sociable, but he's been a bit erratic lately. Funny – he's playing really well on the weekends. Better than ever. Training, not so much. It's like he's been running out of steam."

"That's unusual?" asked the detective.

"Let's say, it's a recent development. I've been concerned that maybe I've been pushing them too hard at training. I've noticed something similar with a couple of others. Not as obvious as Tiki. And come game-time, they've all been fine."

"Was Solomona in that category, too?"

Bill grimaced. "In hindsight, probably yes."

There was an awkward silence as Mulholland considered what she should say next. She decided to trust her instincts about this man.

"Bill, I've already told you, the coroner found drugs in Solomona's system. Unusual drugs."

The coach's healthy tanned skin had paled. "Not steroids, you said."

She shook her head and replied, "No. Something else."

"Did it… whatever it was… did it kill him?"

"No. Well, certainly not directly, like poisoning. It might have affected his behaviour, impaired his judgement, something like that. My question is, has anyone else shown signs of – impairment? Could the behaviours we were just talking about be drug-related? I'm sorry, Bill."

"Me too," Cameron replied. "I'll… have to think about this for a while… But not right now."

"Of course. One last thing, though. Trevor Salmon told me he didn't have much to do with the Demons players, but that's not the impression I got from some of the boys."

"He keeps tabs on the team. Closer with some than with others. He employs a few of them, but, er, keeps it quiet. Cash payments, no tax, as I understand it. I guess that's why he didn't mention it to you. I'm sorry, Rita. I suppose I've taken the attitude, 'ask no questions and get told no lies'. The income means we've kept some players who might otherwise go elsewhere. Or else find even less legal ways of making money, I'm afraid."

Rita nodded. "That makes sense. In theory, I should probably notify the Tax Office, but in my experience, they're not good at sharing information with us. I'll just sit on the information – thanks, Bill."

"That's okay. I'm not trying to get Trevor into trouble. He's committed to the team, and he puts his money where his mouth is. From what I can tell, he's a good businessman. Built up the family wealth. No 'showbiz' about him – he comes across as much more serious than his brother."

"The one who's apparently 'gone walkabout'? Trevor did say something about his artistic temperament," recalled Mulholland.

Bill chuckled. "I only met him once at a post-season event, but that certainly fits with what he sounded like on the radio. They seem to be missing him there, they keep broadcasting 'where's Mike?' type messages."

The detective looked blank. She'd made no connection with

Trevor Salmon's wandering sibling. Neither she nor Bob Sterling listened to CRD-FM. If anyone else in the police station did, they'd made no mention of the missing deejay. And nobody at the radio station had contacted the police.

"Probably not relevant," she said. "I should ask some questions about it though, I suppose. That's enough of business, hey? I really would just like to know a bit more about you – and I promise, not for any professional reasons."

Bill Cameron's smile widened. He was very pleased to hear that, for more than one reason. Solomona's death, and the subsequent enquiries, were weighing heavily on his mind. And he also was rapidly developing a very non-professional interest in Rita Mulholland. It would be nice to forget her occupation just for a little while, if possible.

Tristan's was a good spot for just such a quiet conversation on a Thursday night. For now, the pair were more than happy to simply enjoy each other's company. Stressful considerations could be resumed tomorrow.

.ooo.

14

It was the Friday morning of Jim Cooke's first day as a volunteer guide at Dunbar's Fishing Museum. As planned, Cianawyn and Arthur were going to take Callie to the Museum. The three were in her room in Cromwell House. The elderly Mrs Steele wasn't immobile, but she moved slowly and often painfully. Preparations for 'going out' sometimes took time, hence Cianawyn's insistence on arriving early before departure to their friend's new adventure.

First, though, was the important priority of coffee and a plate of shortbread. As the threesome sipped and ate, Callie was brought up to date on the gossip from CRD-FM.

"Your friend Gordon sounds like he has issues with a few people there," said the matriarch.

"He can be a grumpy sod when the mood takes him," Arthur admitted. "He can also be absolutely charming when he wants to be."

His wife smiled as she agreed, "That's certainly true. I've seen it. Mum, if you'd like to hear what he sounds like for yourself, he should still be on air."

They did indeed catch the tail end of Teller's morning show. As the last strains of Toto's 'Africa' faded, he delivered the day's Community Announcements, then cut to the news.

Like most community radio stations, CRD-FM got their news service from a national provider, so there was no local content. It was the usual mix of politics from home and abroad, extreme weather, and sports. After the bulletin, Gordon gave the local weather forecast, then signed off from his shift. An old Buddy Holly track started, after which the listeners knew to expect a shrill "Hi Fitzroy!" as the elderly deejay took over.

That prospect was enough for Callie to reach out and snap the radio off. "Mutton pretending to be lamb," she said peevishly.

"Gordon reckons Fitzroy's nearly eighty," remarked Arthur.

"Huh! I'm over eighty, but I don't pretend that I'm still anything like the belle of the ball," replied his mother-in-law.

Cianawyn suppressed a giggle at the image crossing her mind. "The joy of radio, Mum. It's not like anyone can actually see him. He quite possibly thinks he really is still a hip groover. Anyway, we should be on our way."

Not very long after, their station wagon pulled into the car park alongside the Dunbar Fishing Museum. A helpful 'Drop-off Zone' by the front door allowed Callie, her folding wheelchair, and her darling daughter to be unloaded at the entrance before Arthur drove off to seek a parking space.

The coastal town of Dunbar had a long history as a centre for fishing, both commercial and recreational. The commercial side had been tapering off for years, due to over-fishing and, more recently, changes in the water temperature and conditions. But it was still a popular spot for amateurs, and anglers made up a good proportion of both the visiting tourists and the retirees who settled in the area.

The Museum itself occupied one of the original boathouses along the Dunbar shoreline. It had been gutted and refurbished, and an extension added to form an L-shape at the rear. For nearly twenty years it had been progressively filled with photographs, equipment (mostly antique) and other memorabilia. Much of it was donated, and occasionally special pieces were bought with the aid of one or more benefactors. Over the years, quite a few of those bene-factors made it on to the Museum's Board, whose names were enshrined on an elegant sign mounted on the wall beside the entrance.

That sign was what Cianawyn and her mother read as they waited for their driver.

"There's one of those odd coincidences we like," observed Cianawyn, pointing.

"What? Oh! I see!" laughed Callie. "The irony of a Salmon being on the Board of the Fishing Museum."

Her daughter didn't quite share the jovial reaction. She sounded thoughtful as she said, "I've heard a few things about Trevor Salmon helping out young people through his business. I guess his being involved in a non-profit enterprise like this would be consistent."

Arthur joined them, getting behind the wheelchair. "Did I hear the Salmon name being bandied about?"

Cianawyn indicated the name on the board, and said, "I'm surprised that Mike's name isn't there alongside his brother's. Just for the sake of publicity."

"Cynical, my darling, but I do take your point," agreed Arthur as he wheeled his mother-in-law into the Museum. "Gordon did mention that Mike did some fishing, but wasn't as keen as his brother."

That thread of conversation was shelved as Arthur placed the "donation" that was the Museum's entry fee into an Honour Box at the front desk. As the threesome made their way into the Museum they were greeted by a wave from Dawn Crane, standing proudly beside the new volunteer guide.

"Hello folks – thank you so much for coming!" said Jim, smiling broadly.

"Our pleasure, young Jim," replied Callie. "Now, sir, do your duty, please, and show us around."

"Um, I've had the tour, but I'd like to see it again, if you don't mind my company?" asked Dawn.

"Of course not! We'd be happy to have you with us," exclaimed Callie, to the quiet delight of both Dawn and Jim.

For the next fifteen minutes or so, Jim Cooke was able to demonstrate how well he'd absorbed his training, as they moved from exhibit to exhibit. Along the way, Callie and her daughter managed to extract from their guide what had prompted him to take on the job.

They knew a little of his history already: that he'd seen service in the Royal Australian Navy, but had his career cut short by an unfortunate accident. It turned out that exposure to a gas leak had left him with a chest condition that meant he was no longer fit for active service.

After that, he'd studied accountancy and made that his career, but always retained his quiet fondness for matters nautical. His affection was really for boats, more than fishing, but the Museum featured a few vessels, big and small, inside and in an outdoor display, as well as paraphernalia from many others.

As the little group made their way out a side door to look at the outdoor exhibits, Cianawyn asked casually, "Jim, do you know anything about Trevor Salmon's connection to the Museum? I know he's on the Board."

"Yes, he happened to drop in on one of my training days. Apparently, he comes in from time to time to look things over. I understand his family was involved in fishing in the early days. They owned a small fleet of trawlers, and only moved into other things when that income went into decline. The Salmons still have the family home in the Dunes, I believe, and still do some boating."

"Probably something a bit more flash than this," remarked Arthur as they looked at an old wooden rescue boat.

"Doubtless," agreed Jim with a smile.

They ambled back inside for a last look around. Even Callie would admit that it had been "quite an interesting experience" for them all. As they casually made their way towards the exit, there was a sudden loud scrabbling from the corrugated iron roof above them. Two seagulls were fighting. Instinctively Cianawyn had looked up for the source of the noise, but then as she lowered her gaze, something caught her eye on one of the wall-mounted displays.

"Wow, that's realistic!" she exclaimed.

"What?" asked Arthur.

His wife pointed. "The bloodstain on that – what's it called – blade thing on the wall."

"Gaff hook," said Arthur, helpfully reading a small sign.

Jim frowned. "Odd – I thought all the exhibits were meant to be clean. I'd better fix it."

The rookie guide lifted the old implement down from its mountings, then patted his pockets for a handkerchief to wipe away the stain.

Looking over his shoulder, Cianawyn suddenly grasped his wrist to stop him. "Er, hang on," she said. "Maybe better not – this doesn't look very old."

"Oh! Oh, indeed, it doesn't," Jim agreed, turning the long-bladed piece over in his hands.

Callie, in her wheelchair, was looking at the gaff hook from a different angle. "It looks to me as though it's been wiped clean, but in a hurry. Someone's missed a bit."

It crossed Cianawyn's mind that it would have been good if Kenneth Derbishire were there, but he and Dolly weren't expected for some time yet. But perhaps his son would be the man to call. She stepped away from the little group into a quiet corner, away from the front door just in case of new arrivals.

The phone number of the Dunbar Police Station was programmed into Cianawyn's mobile, and she was pleased when the answering desk sergeant on duty turned out to be Chris Derbishire.

"Ms. Lauder! Nice to hear your voice. What can I do for you?"

Succinctly, Cianawyn explained their discovery.

"Odd," agreed the sergeant. "Are you sure it's not old fish blood?"

"That's certainly a possibility. But the guide is quite sure all the exhibits are cleaned before they go on display. And Sergeant – how can I put this? I just have a feeling about it. An instinct."

"Past experience tells me to trust your instinct, Ms. Lauder. Get the Museum staff to hold onto the thing, please. I'll come over, pick it up, and get it examined," said Derbishire.

"Thanks. I'll do that. Do you want us to stay here and wait for you?" Cianawyn asked.

"Would you mind? I'll be as quick as I can."

Cianawyn looked over towards her mother's wheelchair. "Thanks," she said, "I'd like to get Mum home for lunch before too much longer."

Sergeant Derbishire was as good as his word. He immediately tapped a constable to take over desk duties, and left a message on Rita Mulholland's desk, briefly outlining where he was going. The detective herself was out of the station, trying to interview people in the local Pacific Islander community. Detective Sergeant Sterling was similarly absent, visiting the police garage where Solomona Tuafeulaki's car was impounded in hopes of fresh clues.

It was hard to know what to make of the discovery at the Fishing Museum. Even once he was there, examining the gaff hook for himself.

It was an antique piece of equipment. A six-foot long wooden pole still bore traces of its original varnish, where that hadn't been worn off by years of handling. Securely attached to one end was a fifteen-inch steel spike that had been fashioned into a shape like a question mark. Intended to stab and drag particularly big, tough fish, the tip of the spike was extremely sharp. The next couple of inches of curved steel on this hook had been filed in such a way as to create a razor-like edge, the better to penetrate hard scales and thick piscine flesh.

The sharp part of the gaff hook was shiny and clean, but it was near its base, where the metal joined the wooden pole, that the anomaly was spotted by Cianawyn's keen eyes. A rust-coloured ring at the bottom of the spike, and what had caught her attention – a similarly hued stain that appeared to have trickled a small way down the top of the wood.

"I have to say, I share your misgivings about this, Ms. Lauder," said the policemen as he wrote down his notes.

He'd already established that none of the other visitors could contribute much to her statement. He did, however, require more information from Jim Cooke. Cianawyn, Arthur and Callie were allowed to go home. Similar permission was offered to Dawn, but she was quietly insistent on remaining at the Museum until Jim's shift finished. She knew Dolly Bertram was due to arrive soon, and with her would be the policeman's father.

Jim explained the Museum's processes as thoroughly as he could. It was, in fact, advantageous that Cooke was new in the job, as all his training was fresh in his mind. There'd been no chance for routine to dull his sense of proper procedure.

Chris wasn't sure how interested the detectives would be in this discovery, given how busy they apparently were with the death of Solomona Tuafeulaki. But his policeman's instincts were aroused, in exactly the same way as Cianawyn Lauder's intuition.

They'd both learned to listen to those little inner voices.

.000.

15

———

When Constable Dave Pierce agreed to take over the desk duties from Sergeant Derbishire for a little while, he'd hoped for a spell of peace and quiet. After all, Dunbar was still mostly an easy-going place to live.

He wasn't quite successful in that. Almost an hour after settling into the chair he had to field an unsettling phone call. Some kids, apparently home from school with the flu, had been walking their dog on Sunrise Beach. They'd let go of the leash, and the dog had run off into an area of rocks. When the spaniel refused to return, they'd clambered after it. The animal's distraction became unpleasantly clear when the children found it with its nose buried deep in a man's body. Managing with some effort to extract the dog, they'd run home. Their breathless, garbled explanation was enough to convince the worried mother to call the police, without checking the story herself.

This left Constable Pierce with a problem. This should be a job for a detective, but both were out of the station. Chris Derbishire was the next most senior, but he was out. Most of the other uniformed police were out manning speed cameras. The only other man in the station was Constable 'Flash Nick' Nicholas. He'd had some disciplinary issues recently, and was emphatically <u>not</u> to be put on the desk.

Would it be appropriate to send him to examine the body with the medical crew? Was there a choice?

Then he got lucky. On his second round of attempting to call everyone senior to him Chris Derbishire answered. The sergeant was just in the process of packing the carefully-wrapped gaff hook into the back of his car. He had his own suspicions about the stains on the implement, which he hoped a laboratory would be able to confirm. He'd noted everything he thought might be relevant: the provenance of the hook itself, who normally handled it, who had access to the Museum and when.

Chris decided he should respond to Pierce's call immediately rather than return to the station. He hated to think how that family might be feeling after the grisly discovery. It wasn't a long drive to Sunrise Beach. He parked outside the modest home, then went in to introduce himself.

Very soon, the children were leading the policeman towards the rocks, this time accompanied by their mother. Realizing that they were near the target, Chris asked the family to wait while he picked his way to what the dog had discovered.

The tide hadn't yet removed the body, which wasn't a pretty sight. After quickly returning to the family to thank them and permit them to go back home, Derbishire sat on one of the larger rocks and waited for the ambulance he knew Pierce had requested.

He hadn't moved the body. He took photos with his phone – luckily, he had a strong stomach. The sea had certainly taken its fill. The face-down body looked to be bloodless. Probably leached by the sea, Chris guessed. There were clear signs of scavenger attack. The right leg was almost completely missing, and there were chunks of flesh missing – probably bitten – from across the back of the torso and shoulders.

It was only when the medical team arrived and carefully turned the fragile corpse over for removal that two things became obvious. The naked figure was obviously male. And there was a long wound that ran from the sternum to the man's groin. Exactly as Arthur Bayer had described.

Mentally, Derbishire kicked himself. He knew he hadn't dismissed Bayer's story as casually as D. S. Sterling would have, but now he wondered if he might have done more, although it was hard to think what.

IT WASN'T long before the corpse was laid out on a table for medical examination. Detective Rita Mulholland sat quietly at a discreet distance while the coroner, Doctor Cartwright, went about her business.

Rita had returned to the station just in time to receive Derbishire's report about the newly-found body. She'd listened to the sergeant, and read his hand-written notes. She'd waited for her senior officer's return. If she expected him to show any interest, she was disappointed. Perhaps, she thought, there was only room in Bob Sterling's mind for one case at a time, especially when he had his own potential connection to it.

"The D. S. gave this pretty short shrift," she told the doctor. "He dismissed it as a shark attack, which we get from time to time. Not police business, he reckoned."

"We do get shark attacks," admitted Cartwright. "Judging by the bite mark around the hip, I'd suspect it was a bull shark that took his leg."

"That's what killed him? A bull shark?"

The coroner shook her head. "Only if you know of a bull shark using a blade. That torso wound can't have come from anything natural, in the sea or on the land. I'll need to examine further, but even now, I'd be willing to bet that long gash was the death wound. And that it happened quite some time before the shark bite. The shark may well have been disappointed by how little blood was in the body – I don't know if they regard blood as an important condiment or not."

Mulholland wrote in the trusty notebook that she was never without. "How long do you think he was in the water?" she asked.

"It's hard to say precisely. It's been a while." The coroner was examining the loose edge of the skin around the belly. "Decomposition in salt water isn't as exact a science as I'd like. Currents, water temperature, they can change things. I'd estimate a minimum of two weeks, probably a bit longer."

"I'll need ID. The face is faintly familiar, but it's pretty badly damaged. It's not a face that newspapers will be keen to publish. What about fingerprints?"

Doctor Cartwright lifted a cold white hand and looked at it closely. "Not in great shape. It looks like fish, or crabs, have been nibbling. We can probably salvage a couple, but certainly not a full set."

Rita smiled thinly. "I'll take what I can get."

She continued to sit quietly while the doctor carried on with her work. The two women had known each other for a couple of years, although in normally quiet Dunbar, there was little call for them to work together closely. The occasional accident investigation, or death by misadventure. Murder, even suspected murder, was something that until recently hadn't been known in the town for a long time.

"Any progress that you're allowed to tell me about on that other case? The young man found at the bottom of High Point?" asked Cartwright as she delicately wielded her scalpel.

"Not much," the detective admitted. "We're trying to follow up on that drug you found, but no joy so far. We – I – have been talking with other people in the football club he belonged to."

"I bet that's been fun," said the coroner drily. Her opinion of 'macho swaggering footballers' was lower and more generalised than even Rita's had been before her interactions with the Demons.

"What you'd expect, for the most part," admitted Mulholland with a sigh. "To be fair, though, a couple of them have been quite pleasant. And the coach is very nice."

Doctor Cartwright looked up from her exploration of her subject's remaining portion of intestine. "Nice? Really? So – you don't think he's involved in the drug angle?"

Rita thought quietly for some moments before replying, "No, I really don't. Bill Cameron is an ex-player himself, one of the old-fashioned ones who studied then had a real job while he was playing. He still does, even though he's a professional coach. He spends a few hours per week as a disability support worker."

Cartwright grunted into a descending colon. "He sounds too good to be true."

"I hope not. I like him."

"I'm getting that impression, yes. Well, I hope you're not disappointed, about the drugs, or anything else."

"Thanks. I really did get the impression he was genuinely surprised at what was in Tuafeulaki's system. He seems too sensible a man to have been telling himself 'nothing to see here' when he knew that wasn't true. He was staunchly anti-drugs, but wasn't strident about it. But he might well have been kept in the dark, while he was believing the best of his players."

Cartwright couldn't help her cynicism. "Mm. There can be a fine line between trust and naivete," she said. "Hmm... the sea water has cleaned out most of these insides, but there are a few traces left in some of the intestinal folds. Hopefully enough for me to run some tests."

"Nothing more for me, then, until you've spent some time staring into a microscope?"

"I'm afraid not," the doctor replied. "Nothing obvious. I'm sorry, it looks like you'll have to go back to your charming boss."

Rita smiled. "Thanks. For your work, and for the conversation."

"My pleasure." The coroner waved her hand over the corpse. "It's nice to talk with someone who actually can talk back. Without scaring the hell out of me."

.ooo.

16

———————

Cianawyn and Arthur were taking their turn at selling tickets in the weekly Old Bastards fund-raising raffle. They made their way around The Watering Hole, Arthur's arms full with an excellent meat tray, a boxed bottle of wine, and a box of good chocolates. His darling bride took care of the ticket sales.

While they were busy, Callie was deep in conversation with Kenneth Derbishire, who'd just arrived. It was a much-depleted table for a Friday night. Dolly Bertram was playing the piano for a school concert. Jim Cooke had taken Dawn out to dinner as a gesture of thanks for her efforts on his first day at the Museum. Even if the police visit had rather taken the gloss off the occasion.

"My boy Chris called me late this afternoon," Kenneth explained. "Seems like young Arthur has been proved right. A body like he described has been found washed up on Sunrise Beach."

"Sunrise Beach? That's quite a way from where we were," observed Cailleach.

"I know. It's odd. But Chris is quite sure that the corpse they found matches the description your son-in-law gave him. Allowing for some more time in the water. I'll tell Arthur about it when he and Cianawyn get back to the table."

Callie smiled. "I'm sure he'll be pleased. I know he doesn't like it when his word is doubted."

"None of us do, Callie," he replied, returning the smile. "Chris mentioned another thing. Something he picked up at the Fishing Museum."

"I know. I was there. A blade thing used in sea fishing, and a body washed up with a big long cut in it. Do you believe in coincidence, Kenneth?"

"About as much as you do," answered the retired policeman.

The raffle drawn, Cianawyn and Arthur bought a round of drinks and returned to the table. There, they were brought up to date by the other two. Cianawyn immediately joined the dots just as her mother had done. Her husband was just about as quick.

"I wonder if Mr. Sterling will make the same connection that we did?" mused Cianawyn.

Derbishire gave a short laugh. "I doubt it. In fact, do you know what Chris said his reaction to the body was? He reckoned it was a skinny dipper that a shark got."

"Not if it's the same body that I saw," said Arthur.

"Arthur, would you be able – willing, to look at the corpse?" asked Kenneth.

"It's not a pleasant prospect, but I've survived it once, so yes."

"Would you mind if I had a word with my boy and organized for you to have a look on Monday?"

"Go ahead," agreed Bayer. "But isn't this a bit out of his pay grade?"

"Agreed. By rights, the request should come from a detective. But I've told you Bob Sterling's attitude," said Derbishire.

"I'm afraid he's right," said Cianawyn. "What about Detective Mulholland?"

Derbishire shrugged. "I've heard the name."

"She's a very sensible woman," said Callie. "I – we – had a bit to do with her a little while ago. Please ask your son to have a word with her."

Kenneth readily agreed.

The four talked quietly about what little they knew of the strange situation. The more they talked, the more they were aware of the questions. Who was the dead man? Why was he murdered? (None of them doubted that was the cause of death.) How had he come to wash up at Cemetery Beach, and then again, later, at Sunrise Beach? Who were the two strangers Arthur had met on the rainy beach? If they'd never contacted the police as they'd promised (which seemed likely), why not? Laziness? Or something more sinister?

"While we're talking about mysteries, and Dolly isn't here, can I share some things I've heard in the dressing room? I'd appreciate your thoughts," said Cianawyn.

At the nods of the other three, she went on to explain the stories and suspicions she'd heard backstage, mostly about Mike Salmon, but also referencing his brother Trevor.

"One thing that puzzles me," she said, "I don't understand why, if Mike has been missing for weeks, there seems to have been nothing heard from his brother. No public appeals, or anything like that. In which case, does <u>he</u> know where Mike is?"

"In which case, why isn't he telling anyone? A reasonable question, dear," agreed her mother.

Arthur shrugged. "Not all siblings are close, darling, from what I understand. Personally, I wouldn't know…"

"You're right," agreed Kenneth, "I'm lucky. I've always gotten on well with my brother, and all three of my kids are friends. But not all families are like that. I do know that the Salmons are an old Dunbar family – there's an old family home over at the Dunes."

"We know. And we understand that both brothers fish," said Arthur. "Maybe not together, though. That could be why it's only Trevor who's on the Museum Board."

Cianawyn was still musing on dressing room conversations. "One thing they seem to do together is convince young people to move to Sydney. Mike wins them over to the idea, and his brother is apparently the facilitator."

She explained what had happened to Georgie Fletcher, and the invitations or suggestions made to others.

Nobody at the table could add much to the consideration. Arthur had managed to avoid Sydney for most of his life. Callie and Kenneth had both spent considerable time there, but neither had had anything to do with the older Salmon brother. They knew the Sage-Corp name – the development company had a significant profile – but their knowledge was confined to what had been in the newspapers.

"I just can't help thinking there's something fishy about them," said Cianawyn.

"About the Salmons? That sounds like something I'd have said," observed her husband.

Callie nodded. "It does indeed. But that doesn't make it less true."

.ooo.

17

———————

Overtime wasn't something that Rita Mulholland did often, or without good reason.

The message from Doctor Cartwright just before 5:00p.m. counted as a good reason, as far as she was concerned.

The coroner had managed to lift three almost complete fingerprints from the sea-damaged corpse. Immersion had made the task difficult, but the doctor was persistent. Eventually, she'd been able to get those prints onto a card – a card which she'd immediately sent to her friend, the detective. Cartwright had no faith in the Detective Sergeant's willingness to go to much effort in this case. Not until he thought it would be career-enhancing.

Rita, on the other hand, was very prepared to put time in to find answers. The Tuafeulaki case was very much open still, but there seemed little more that could be done in the short term. The bloodless body on the beach had her intrigued. Cartwright's latest note said that she was "pursuing a further line of enquiry", which suggested that her curiosity was as piqued as the detective's own.

The computer system at Dunbar Police Station was sufficiently well equipped for Mulholland to access a comprehensive file of recorded fingerprints, but not for her to scan the card and let the computer do the work. As a result of which, she sat at her terminal, scrolling through pictures of loops, whorls and arches, comparing them with those on the card.

It was a slow process, and taxing on the eyes. After three hours, those eyes were sore, and the vision they provided was starting to waver. Coffee. It was coffee or quit, and she wasn't willing to quit. She'd set herself a task and she was going to finish it. If possible, of course. There was no guarantee that this John Doe's prints were on file in the State, or anywhere else for that matter, but it was the only database she could access to follow this particular possible lead. Maybe her D. S. could authorize access to other States' information, if he could be convinced of the value, but she hoped it wouldn't come to that.

Maybe it was the power of positive thinking, or perhaps Rita's luck was simply due for a change. Less than ten minutes after finishing the (typically terrible) coffee she found a match.

Some years earlier, there'd been a break-in at a home on the outskirts of Dunbar. Residents and regular visitors had all been fingerprinted so as to exclude them from prints found at the scene. Among those prints were the three she'd been looking for. They were from the fingers of Mike Salmon.

ON THE OTHER side of town from the Salmon family's prestigious old beach house was the modestly well-to-do area of Dunbar Heights.

At the same time that Cianawyn and Arthur were starting to sell raffle tickets, a dozen or so men were starting to gather at what was normally a quiet two-story brick home in Dunbar Heights. They'd assembled in the downstairs 'recreation room' (read: a lounge with bar and large-screen TV) for a special occasion.

The 'man of the house', Dan Markham, was hosting a "good old-fashioned Buck's Night" for his son Mitch, due to be married on the coming Sunday. Dan, a builder, had invited several of his buddies, while Mitch's guests were his friends from University. The catering was party pies, frozen pizzas, and kegs of beer. The entertainment was music (loud) and movies (blue).

The latter were provided by one of Dan's regular plumbing contractors, Roo. He, in turn, had obtained them from the man who ultimately gave employment to most of the men there from the building trade – Trevor Salmon. The boss of SageCorp wasn't attending the event himself. He tended to move in different circles, where there was more money around, or where he had control of the guest list.

The porn film industry is a truly international one. The first short movie of the evening had been made in Sweden, the next in the USA. After a short break for more beer and pizza, movie #3 rolled onto the big screen. This one was an Australian production, from a small Sydney studio.

Not unusually for the genre, there was little in the way of plot, or storyline. An apparently wealthy young man (with the obligatory moustache) hung around in his apartment as a succession of beautiful women came and sometimes went to share their affections with him.

The third young lady to appear was the youngest of the parade, blonde and pretty. And for some of this audience – one in particular – familiar.

Neil Fletcher sat staring, open-mouthed, not even able to answer when Dan nudged him and asked quietly, "Isn't that your daughter?"

Numbly, he managed to nod. Diplomatically, his host grabbed the remote control and hit Fast Forward. Fletcher's brain was spinning, and not just from several beers. This was the 'great career opportunity' she'd gone to Sydney for? That she'd been lured there for?

Mike Salmon – he'd been the one responsible. He'd sent Georgie to Sydney with stars in her eyes. 'Contacts' he'd said. 'Contacts in the industry', but not the industry the Fletchers had expected. Not Neil or Mary, nor, he was sure, Georgie herself. Mary – how would he tell Mary? Could he tell Mary?

Some of the party-goers had already turned their attention back to the screen. Another Scandinavian offering was now showing. A

few, though, were watching Neil Fletcher with concern. The hardware store owner's face had gone very pale after his initial deep flush
of embarrassment.

Cautiously, Dan Markham leaned close to his old friend. "Neil?
Are you okay? Can I call a taxi for you, mate? Get you home? I'm so
sorry, mate, I had no idea. This must be a helluva shock..."

"Yeah. Yeah. Thanks," Fletcher mumbled.

The call made, Markham waited silently on the footpath beside
the stunned father.

This was what had come of involvement in the theatre. He and
Mary should never have gone along with it. No wonder they'd heard
nothing from Georgie for a while. They'd have to go to Sydney. Find
her. Rescue her.

But would she even want that? Who knows what had been done
to her, to even get her into such a situation?

And the business? Could he, or Mary, far less both, afford to be
away from the store for an undetermined period of time? Of course
Georgie's welfare was more important – but business was so parlous
at the moment. Even a couple of weeks without income could be the
finish of them. What would be the point of finding Georgie if there
was nothing to bring her home to?

"Neil? Neil? Your cab's here, mate!" prompted Dan.

"Eh? Oh! Ah, thanks. I'll... er... I'll see you..."

"Sure. Sure, mate. You just call if you need me, eh? And I'm really
sorry I –"

"Skip it, Dan. Not your fault. I'll... Well, I'll deal with it."

With those parting words, Fletcher got into the taxi and headed
homeward.

'I wonder what he meant by that?' thought Markham. He
shrugged and slowly went back into the party, which had lost some of
its appeal.

.ooo.

18

———————

Saturday afternoons had become rehearsal time, as *Sweeney Todd*'s Opening Night crept closer. Cianawyn was there because of a couple of final fittings she still had to do.

Tom Beaumaris' madhouse keeper's uniform was proving trickier than anticipated. Shauna had wanted a very particular style of coat for him, and the broad shoulders of the ex-rower were proving challenging.

He arrived in the dressing room in high spirits. It required no prompting for him to reveal that only this morning he and had wife had proudly handed the keys to the promised car over to their son Ted.

"I'm so proud of him for getting that apprenticeship," he enthused. "Oh sure, I might have wanted him to pursue something more academic, once. But that's just not the way the young feller's wired, and Laura and I just have to respect that."

"That's a very sensible approach," agreed Cianawyn warmly. "Please give him my congratulations. I'm sure his friends Nick and Zoe and Nathan will be pleased, too."

"Oh yes. The Rankins are good kids. Nathan Finnegan's alright, too. He and Ted used to be really good mates, but I think they've drifted apart a bit lately."

"That's a shame. It happens with kids, though – I remember it happened with me after I left school."

Tom smiled. "Quite right, Miz Lauder." He was another who'd decided to avoid mispronouncing the distinctive Welsh name. "I think it's got something to do with the job. Something they disagree about. Ah well, it'll all blow over, or it won't. They do seem to still get on alright, and Ted's very happy, which is the most important thing."

"Well said," agreed the seamstress. "Now, try moving your arms. Can you roll your shoulders?"

"How's this? It feels comfortable now, thank you."

"Good – it still sits a little awkwardly, I'm afraid," she admitted.

"Jarvis Fogg is a pretty awkward character," replied the actor. "It's probably appropriate."

"Ha, I hope Shauna agrees with you!"

"I'll win her over, don't you worry. The mood I'm in, even Shauna and Adeline Bond combined couldn't take the smile off my face!"

Very soon he was back out to rehearse, his broad grin adding a nice twist to his villainous character. Cianawyn flexed her own shoulders, ready for her final 'customer'.

Jasper Oakley – Darryl Frankem, the vet, had missed a few rehearsals. Shauna hadn't been too worried: Darryl had let her know in advance, his role wasn't large, and she'd worked with him before, thus knew he could be relied on to get his lines and movements right.

His green vest and striped trousers had yet to be adjusted to suit, however. He wasn't a tall man, and the wardrobe mistress wanted to be sure she'd correctly accounted for the length (or lack thereof) of his torso and legs.

"It's alright," she'd reassured him when he came in after the regular warm-up. "Someone has to be last."

As Cianawyn knelt at his feet, pinning the hem of the trousers, Darryl said casually, "You've been asking about Mike, I hear."

Cianawyn looked up in surprise. There was nothing threatening about the voice – indeed, Frankem sounded almost charming. Perhaps that was what surprised her.

"Yes," she replied, "I'm just curious about why someone who apparently loved performing would walk away from a lead role, when they've never had one before."

"Well, heh heh, maybe he got a better offer, and was too embarrassed to tell anyone."

Lauder raised her eyebrows. "That's an interesting thought. I wonder if his brother knows anything about it."

"I can guarantee you that he doesn't," said Darryl casually.

That was a surprise. "How?"

"I work with Trevor a lot, and we talk," he explained.

Cianawyn was puzzled. "I thought he was a builder. You're a vet, aren't you, Darryl?"

"Yes, that's right. And Trevor has a number of racing greyhounds that I look after for him, especially when he's away in Sydney."

"I see." She continued to pin and fold in thoughtful silence.

"Why your interest in our lost lead?" asked Frankem.

As she got to her feet, and made a last adjustment to the green vest, Cianawyn made sure she sounded as casual in her reply. "Like I said, just curious. I haven't had much experience in the theatre, except as an audience. To an outsider, it seems strange to have someone in a starring role just quit, without saying anything to anyone."

"Yes. Yes, I can understand that," was the thoughtful reply. "I'm afraid I don't know Mike anywhere near as well as his brother. I think he's always been a bit of a strange cove. I could say 'all actors are', but I guess I'd be condemning myself then, eh?"

They both laughed lightly before Darryl continued. "Tell you what, I _will_ ask Trevor next time I see him. He and his brother aren't what you'd call close, but maybe they had an argument or something, and Mike went away to cool off. It's not like Trevor would tell me for any reason – none of my business."

"Even with you and Mike being in the show together?" said Cianawyn, surprised.

Darryl shrugged. "Trevor's interest in the theatre is about zero," he replied. "I don't know that he's ever even been to a show that Mike's been in. Are you all done with me?"

"Yes – I am, thanks."

"Good. Nice to chat. See you later," he said as he left the dressing room.

'That was interesting,' mused Cianawyn to herself. 'He's polite - friendly, even, and everything he said seemed quite reasonable. So why am I feeling suspicious?'

At the front of the stage, Shauna nodded in satisfaction as Darryl rejoined the ensemble.

"Okay, let's run through Act One, Scene Three. Adeline, watch the first run-through for me, please. Take notes, but don't interrupt. I want to have a quick word with Shan."

With that, she made her way backstage, soon allowing herself to drop heavily onto a chair near her wardrobe mistress.

"All set now?" she asked.

Cianawyn nodded as she sat down herself, and patted the exercise book she'd been using.

"Two-thirds, maybe almost three-quarters, of all the outfits are ready. And I've got all the details I need to finish the rest," she said.

"Excellent," the director replied, and turned to look at the costumes hanging on their racks across the dressing room's back wall. "That colour theme idea has worked well," she observed.

With some difficulty, she struggled to haul herself up off the chair to examine some of the clothes more closely. Cianawyn knew better than to offer any assistance. Shauna knew her body shape was awkward, but she'd made her own lifestyle choices and determinedly took responsibility for them. But she did curse as, just as she stood, her mobile phone rang.

"Bugger," the director growled as she dropped back down on the chair. "Shauna Shallacot, hello... who? Mary! Oh, sorry – I didn't recognize your number. It's usually Neil who calls. Is everything okay? I... What? Hang on, slow down, I..."

There was a pause from Shauna, while the electronic crackle of

Mary Fletcher's voice was just below what Cianawyn could clearly make out. She had to settle for reading Shallacot's face, but that was telling her plenty.

"No, Mary, I... yes, yes. Oh, absolutely I understand your concern. But can I just say..."

Another pause. The crackle of Mary's voice was audible again, barely. It continued for a while.

"Oh, Mary, it's awful. But I... we... yes. He's not with us any more, you understand? No. No, of course. I... I can't blame you. I'm very, very sorry, Mary. Please do call if there's anything I can do... of course... no..."

Abruptly the line went dead. Shauna sighed. A deep exhalation that seemed to well from the very centre of her substantial figure.

"What's happened?" asked Cianawyn, cautiously.

After another sigh, the director related all that Mary Fletcher had told her. That she and her husband were quitting the Dunbar & District Players, effective immediately, and why. In detail, Mary had explained why neither of them could ever set foot in the Terrence Theatre again – what Neil had seen, how they blamed the Salmon brothers and the acting profession in general – 'it was such an unreal environment'. How they wanted to go to Sydney to look for Georgie, but admittedly had no idea where to start.

"I'm very sorry for them, naturally," said Shauna. "But for me, too. I've got to find two more actors from somewhere, and we start dress rehearsals in just over a week!"

Her mind turning over the Fletchers' sad story, Cianawyn replied vaguely, "Maybe someone can double up roles?"

"Very tricky for timing. You'd have to redesign some of those lovely Victorian costumes for ultra-quick changes. Say – wait on. You've been at plenty of rehearsals. Mrs Poorlean isn't a big role, Will Marlow is competent enough to help you if you lose a line."

"I'm not an actress," Cianawyn protested.

Shauna gestured dismissively. "What is it your husband says when dealing with Adeline? 'We're just props that talk.' You'll manage, I'm sure. And you'll find it much easier to adapt Mary's costume to your size than mine."

The fate of Georgie Fletcher was still at the front of the wardrobe mistress's mind, so it was almost an automatic response when she replied, "Yes, that makes sense, okay."

It was only later, standing on stage with a script in her hand, that she properly realized what she'd just let herself in for.

As if she didn't already have enough to concentrate on!

.ooo.

19

Only a month earlier, if someone had asked Rita Mulholland, "are you going to the football on Saturday?" she would have stared at them as if they were insane. She was as likely to attend a rugby league game as she was to perform a triple back-somersault from a standing start, and not on a diving board. Yet here she was at Tate Park, watching the Dunbar Demons in pitched battle against the might of the Burrawidgee Budgies.

The home team wore black armbands – really strips of black electrical tape around bulging biceps – in memory of Solomona Tuafeulaki. The one-page match program even included a paragraph acknowledging his passing. No details at all, Rita was pleased to see, but an apparently sincere expression of regret at the loss of a friend, talented footballer, and "a fine young man who impressed all who knew him". She had a hunch that Bill Cameron was responsible for the words.

But there was no melancholy affecting the game, for either team. The Budgies, resplendent in green and yellow, were making a decent go of standing up to the local heroes. Slightly lighter, man-for-man, than the Demons, their speed was enabling them to stay competitive so far. There were five minutes to go in the first half, and the red-and-blue Demons led by ten points to six.

The colours were important to Rita. She knew the faces of the Dunbar players if they stood still long enough, but at speed she had no chance. At least the very different jerseys allowed her to tell the two teams apart, so she wouldn't embarrass herself by cheering for the wrong side.

In 'civvies' – a denim skirt, plain red shirt and a broad-brimmed straw hat, it was unlikely that Bob Sterling would recognize her, even if he did chance to look over from the Members' Bar to the rather rickety old stand at the car park end of the ground.

Club rumour had it that Trevor Salmon was offering to co-fund the construction of a new stand, <u>if</u> the government would match him dollar-for-dollar. There were a couple of potential problems with this idea, though. One was that their local Member of Parliament didn't belong to the party currently in power. Nor was it a marginal electorate, so the chances of securing support from the corridors of power seemed remote.

Secondly, it was widely (although unofficially) recognized that Trevor's support would be contingent upon his firm getting the construction contract. This meant that the money would be going back to him anyway. And there was also the strong suspicion that the costing figures would be as rubbery as a kids' trampoline, so Trev would be turning a very good profit on his 'charitable offer'. Not everyone in the community, even the football club community, approved of that.

So, for now, the forty-something-year-old timber framed stand remained the only option for non-member spectators who didn't want to stand or sit on the patchy dry grass. It didn't bother Rita. She still had a decent view. To be honest, even that might be fairly unimportant given her limited understanding of the game and its rules.

But what Rita <u>was</u>, was a shrewd observer, and listener. She may not know much about the technicalities of the game, but she understood behaviours and body language. She also paid attention to the comments, constructive or otherwise, of the small crowd around her.

There were perhaps 120 people at the ground, and less than thirty of them were braving the not-so-grandstand. But they were a vocal little enclave, and the detective's education in "the greatest game of all" was advancing rapidly.

She already knew that referees were among the only people in the community held in lower esteem than police and parking inspectors. And of course, it was expected that opposition players would be on the end of plenty of vitriol. What she hadn't expected, though, was the level of criticism thrown at Dunbar's own. Mistakes were heckled quickly and loudly, and not always reasonably, as far as Rita could see. Certain players, she noticed, were treated more harshly than others.

There were a few people in her vicinity who levelled much of their criticism at the Demons' coach. Her automatic reaction was to round on them, particularly the really abusive ones, but she resisted. She realized the futility of it, especially when she knew she'd be acting out of loyalty, not actually knowing if the criticism was in any way fair. It did her heart good, though, when others in the stand took umbrage at a couple of fierce, abusive critics.

The raucous pair were told in no uncertain terms that they had absolutely no chance of doing a better job than Bill Cameron. Some creative suggestions were made as to what they could do with their criticisms. Rita's own favourite was the advice to write the offending comments on a length of rough cut 2x4 timber, then insert that timber "where the sun doesn't bloody shine".

Actually, it was very much cruder than that, but Rita had been raised quite demurely and automatically edited the expression in her head. That said, her own thought had been that the length of timber should be applied forcefully to the head of the loud offensive man. Repeatedly. But she didn't say that out loud. It did help her to realize, though, just how fond of the Demons' coach she'd already become.

That fondness was a part of the reason for her being there. Unofficially, she was watching the conduct of several Persons of Interest in the Tuafeulaki case. Detective Sergeant Sterling wouldn't have agreed to it being an official observation. Protective in equal parts of his club and his overtime budget, she thought.

Her growing affection for Bill, still a closely guarded secret, had already led her to privately dismiss him as a suspect. Anything that she could learn which might bolster that dismissal would be welcome, and a game was an environment where just such evidence might appear. She hoped.

The half time whistle blew, with the score still at 10-6 the Demons' way. The players trooped off in the direction of their dressing rooms. Mulholland's eye was caught by an unexpected movement. A little bit of push and shove – not between opponents, but by three or four players in red and blue.

Some sort of dissension in the ranks, she thought. 'Maybe it happens all the time? I'm sure Bill will sort it out if there _is_ a problem.'

She glanced up into the Members' area to see if anyone there had noticed. It didn't look much like it. Bob Sterling, for example, was nowhere to be seen. A few faces were turned towards the field, and apparently in conversation. One of those was the face of Trevor Salmon. He appeared, from this range, attentive but unconcerned.

Unconcerned. That triggered a recollection. Earlier that morning, Rita had contacted Bob Sterling and revealed the identity of the washed-up corpse.

His first response: "Oh." Then a long silence.

"We did have a fair idea that he was missing, sir," she'd said.

"A suspicion, at best," he'd replied. "No Missing Person report, which is the most important thing."

"Agreed, sir. No Missing Person notification, and now he turns up dead, in very suspicious circumstances."

"A bit strange, perhaps, but we do get shark attack victims along this coast quite often," Sterling had replied.

"But this wasn't a shark attack, not as cause of death. The coroner is absolutely sure of that," Rita had answered, angrily.

"Alright, alright. But we still have nothing to go on."

"What about the brother? He…"

"Yes. He'll have to be told, obviously."

The Detective Sergeant had cut her off too quickly for Rita's comfort.

"Well, yes, but..."

Sterling talked over the top of her. "The question is, when? The Demons have a big home game today. I know Trev... Mr. Salmon, will be there. I understand that there'll be a few significant people, both from Dunbar and other places – I'll be frank, some potential investors from Sydney. I think, Detective, that there is no obvious point in distracting him with this information right now. It can wait until Monday."

For a moment or two, Rita had been silent. Her perspective was very different to that of her superior officer. And yet... she could justify the same conclusion. On Monday, Rita could easily be present to watch the elder Salmon brother's reaction to the news, and especially, his reaction when asked to formally identify Mike's body. Yes. That would be worth watching.

And now Trevor _was_ watching the field, with at least some interest. If he had any thoughts at all of his missing brother, he certainly wasn't showing them. It suddenly dawned on the detective that it might be useful to be closer to the action. The places adjoining the Members' area were 'standing only', but in more than ten years of policing, Rita had spent plenty of time on her feet. Another forty minutes or so wouldn't hurt her.

Determinedly casual, she made her way down from the stand, and strolled around the perimeter of the ground.

A stop at the pie tent for a light lunch. Her expectations weren't high, but the first bite was a delightful surprise. These weren't frozen pies that had been bunged into an oven. These were labours of love, made by the Tate Park Ladies' Auxiliary. This pie that Rita had casually taken a bite of was, quite frankly, superb. Good chunks of good quality beef. An excellent gravy, seasoned beautifully. Light, flaky pastry on top and satisfying not-too-solid-but just-right pastry for the case. Wow!

Rita turned to the older lady who'd just served her, and said exactly that. "Wow! This is, I think, <u>the</u> best, most exquisite pie I've ever eaten!"

"Thanks, dearie. We like 'em."

"Where do you get them from?" Thankfully, the rush had momentarily died down, so Mulholland could engage in a brief conversation.

"Oh, we make 'em ourselves, pet. None o' them frozen rubbish."

"Simply superb, thank you! I'm amazed nobody's tried to buy your recipe!"

"Oh, they 'ave," tutted the lady. "Young Trevor Salmon up there, for instance, he offered quite a bit for what he called 'the rights' to make 'em. But we wouldn't budge. We make 'em ourselves, every week when there's a game on here at Tatey, whatever grade's playin'. Won't have 'em sold anywhere else. They're <u>our</u> pies, they is."

"And they're excellent!"

"Ta, pet. Always nice to hear. Y'know, that bugger tried to say that because we sell 'em here, the recipe prop'ly belongs to the Club. Luckily, the rest of the Committee stood up to 'im. I reckon he's a greedy bugger."

"Really? Interesting. Thanks again," said Rita, standing aside to let the next wave of customers satisfy their appetites.

Mulling over this latest observation on T. Salmon's character, she completed her leisurely stroll to the spot alongside the Members' area. Clutching the remains of her pie, and a can of soft drink – it was an Unlicenced area of the park – she fitted in quite well. The red shirt and blue skirt added to the effect, albeit unintentionally.

Two or three fans stood in front of her, so she couldn't actually lean on the fence to watch as the players ran out at the sound of the siren. But it was a much closer view, she had to admit. Without the height of the stand, such as it was, she had even less perception of the to-and-fro, back-and-forth of the game. However, there was a much more intense, more visceral appreciation of its action and dynamics. Not least, because on-field noises – voices, grunts, and the sound of colliding bodies, were much more audible at this range.

There was also a much clearer view of Bill Cameron and the team bench, over to her right. If that mattered. Which, of course, professionally, it did not. He didn't look worried, just very intensely focussed. Well, that was to be expected of a coach, especially a good one.

Very early in the second half, the Demons were given a penalty for an infringement that Rita neither saw nor understood, even with the vocal enthusiasm of those around her. Daniel Latukefu took the kick, calmly slotting the ball between the uprights with apparent ease to extend Dunbar's lead to 12 – 6.

As the teams ran back into position, though, Daniel's brother Jonah didn't look pleased, despite the additional two points. He was glaring at the Budgies players, and even some of his own teammates.

The detective wasn't the only one to notice. Bill was making "calm down" gestures from the sideline. As team captain, Daniel tried to reinforce that message. He laid a placatory hand on his brother's shoulder, only to have it shrugged off with a snarl. There was a definite air of caution about Daniel as he backed off.

One or two of the more perceptive watchers spotted it too. A fan near Rita remarked to his young companion, "Jeez – Jonah's taken his angry pills today!"

"Too right, Lyle. He's worse than usual."

"Yeah," agreed Lyle. "Been getting this way for a few weeks now, I reckon."

"Yeah. He's a mug."

As ever, Rita made a mental note of the exchange. It would all be transferred to her trusty notebook later.

Several more minutes elapsed, and the trouble escalated. Burrawidgee were given a penalty for a rough tackle by Jonah Latukefu. All but the most one-eyed of Dunbar supporters, like Alfie Hansell, acknowledged that it was a fair call.

"Bloody lucky he's still on the field," was Lyle's observation.

The penalty allowed the Budgies to move from deep in their own territory to fifteen metres from the home side's try-line. A quick pass was thrown to a charging green-and-yellow forward. He burst past one flat-footed defender, then through another lamentably poor attempted tackle, and scored a try that would be easily converted to level the scores.

The offending second defender, Ronny Lofton, was admittedly caught off balance by the speedy Burrawidgee play, but it didn't look good. Jonah told him so, too, loudly and angrily. Jogging back towards his own half, the try scorer grinned and said pleasantly, "Don't take it so hard, mate."

No one was prepared for Latukefu's response. He spun on the balls of his feet and planted his fist hard on the side of the man's face. The crack of a jaw breaking was all too audible even off the field, and a gasp of shock went around many of the fans. (The ageing bootboy, of course, shouted, "Good on yer, son!")

The referee blew his whistle with all the force he could muster, even as Jonah looked to plant a kick in the ribs of his fallen opponent. Ronny grabbed his teammate and pulled him away, aided by Daniel who'd sprinted over immediately.

A cluster of players quickly formed into a melee, Budgies players rushing to defend one of their own, and hard-heads from both sides eager for "a bit of biffo", as an older generation of fans and commentators called deliberate violence. 'Biffo', though, had no place in the modern game of rugby league, and the referee almost blew the pea out of his whistle trying to restore order.

The two team captains, both sensible young men, did a good job of settling matters quickly. Antagonists were separated, and Jonah was soon left standing alone. He was ordered off the field by the referee, who stood at what he hoped was a safe distance, clearly prepared for another explosion of temper.

It didn't happen, though. Latukefu's shoulders slumped. He suddenly looked like a deflated balloon. Mumbling something incomprehensible he trudged off, oblivious to the taunts of both opposition fans and his own team's, irate at now being a man down.

During the break in play, members of both teams had gathered in little groups to calm down, recapture their focus, and discuss the sudden, shocking display of violence.

Two in particular were near the touchline, a little way from the fascinated detective.

"Bloody Major Happy," growled Phil Duff.

"Shut up, you idiot!" snapped Ronny Lofton.

"Well, that's where the bloody blame lies," retorted Duff defensively. "Never during a game. You and I know that. Jonah's a damned fool!"

"So are you if you don't keep your mouth shut!"

"Aw, Bill can't hear me way over hear," Duff protested.

Lofton almost slapped him, but managed to hold back. "No, but you dunno who else can!"

Rita could. "Who's Major Happy?" she asked Lyle.

The man shrugged. "New one on me," he replied. "Maybe it's a nickname for Jonah."

An ironic nickname, Rita mused, like redheads called Bluey, or hulks called Tiny. Plausible, she supposed, but something in her head said it was unlikely. Especially given the tenor of the fleeting conversation she'd caught.

She looked up at the window of the Members' Bar. No sign of Trevor Salmon. Coincidence? Turned away in dismay or disgust or disappointment?

Looking back along the touchline, she saw Bill Cameron say a few terse words to Jonah. The disgraced player was almost shuffling as he as he made his way to the changing room. He was being accompanied by a large, curly-haired man wearing a stretched Dunbar team t-shirt.

'Must be another ex-player, before he ran to so much fat,' Rita thought to herself. 'One I haven't met.'

Interestingly, being a player down actually seemed to inspire the Demons. Their focus, and their discipline, improved markedly. By the games end, they'd run in two more tries, only one of which Daniel converted. Their defence had held admirably firm, too, responding quickly and effectively to Burrawidgee's attacks. The final score of 22-12 was a fair result, as well as a popular one with the home crowd. Nonetheless, Jonah's actions had taken some of the gloss off the win.

Only a few locals actually gloated at the visiting fans. More were genuinely apologetic. That was Bill Cameron's attitude, too, as he commiserated with the Budgies' coach.

"I can't explain it," he admitted. "Jonah's always played hard, but that was completely over the top. I hope your guy's okay."

"I doubt it. My wife's taken him straight to the hospital, and I'll get there as soon as I can. Pretty sure his jaw's broken. The only question is, how bad?"

"I'm afraid you're right," admitted Bill, sadly. "Take my card. If there's anything our Club, or I, can do to help, please call me."

"You can start by keeping that mad bastard off the field," said the opposition coach bitterly.

"I expect that there'll be a suspension that'll take care of that for a while anyway. But yes, I think the Club should certainly take some disciplinary action. Put it this way, mate – I certainly will, and I expect they'll support me."

"Fair enough. I hope so."

With a handshake, the men parted ways.

Cameron was about to head into the changing room when a familiar face caught his eye. He rushed over, and only a last-moment burst of propriety stopped him from catching Rita in an embrace. (She wouldn't have minded.)

"You came to a game!" he exclaimed. "I thought you didn't <u>like</u> football!"

"It's <u>your</u> team. I thought I'd be supportive," she said, diplomatically not mentioning any ulterior, professional motives. "Congratulations on the win."

"Thanks. I'm sorry about the... incident..."

"No need to apologize, Bill. I'm sure it wasn't your fault in any way. I gather from the people who were around me that Jonah has a reputation as a bit of a hothead."

"Sometimes," Bill admitted. He <u>has</u> been getting worse lately. I'm just about to go in and lay the law down to him."

"Ironic, since that's what he's studying."

"Not very successfully, I think. I'd better go. Shall I see you in the bar later on?"

"Hmm – perhaps not. I see enough of my boss at work. I don't want to find myself stuck with him now."

"Understandable. Tonight maybe? That same bar that we went to last time?"

"Tristan's? Great idea," said Rita. "Say, 7:30? Time for us both to wind down, go home, and change?"

"Perfect. It's a date – oh, sorry! I mean..."

"No, it's alright. That's exactly what it is."

They shared smiles. As the coach started to turn away, the detective stopped him.

"One thing, Bill. Who is Major Happy?"

Cameron looked puzzled for a moment, then laughed. "No idea. You tell me. Crowd nickname maybe? A witty one if it is."

"Just something I heard. Don't worry about it. See you tonight."

"I'm looking forward to it," he replied.

They both were. By 7:30 they would both be needing to indulge in happier, less complicated thinking.

.ooo.

20

It was Monday morning, and Trevor Salmon had called a meeting. Not on SageCorp premises. This wasn't SageCorp business. He sat at the head of the dining table in the Dunes beach house which his family had owned for over forty years.

Also at the table were his invitees: Darryl Frankem, Ronny Lofton, Ronny's brother Jonny, and big Graeme Mount. The latter three looked particularly uncomfortable. Trevor wasn't raging or shouting, and that only made it worse.

"That was embarrassing, men," he said quietly. "I had some influential friends up there with me on Saturday. I'd assumed that a game against Burrawidgee, challenging but very win-able, would be a fine opportunity to show off the effectiveness of our product. Overrun a good, game opposition as a couple of lads played above themselves, with our help. Perhaps a contract opportunity for one or two of them, too. And what do I get? A debacle. One of our players, one who I'd specifically told them to keep an eye on, completely loses his grip, and levels one of the opposition. In full view of the referee, and everyone else in Tate Park."

Frankem frowned. "I wasn't there, but I did warn you – warned everyone – that it might sometimes cause a rush of blood. Exacerbating the more primal instincts is the whole point, and for some people especially, the instinct to fight is one of those."

"I do realize that, Darryl," said Salmon, nodding slowly. "I did make it clear that game days were always to be kept 'clean', didn't I?"

All four men nodded vigorously.

"So, what happened?"

"A build-up in his system?" asked Jonny uncertainly.

Daryl Frankem shook his head. "Unlikely. That could happen over time, admittedly. It's hard to predict any individual's behaviour with certainty. Everyone has their own unique metabolism and body chemistry. But Jonah's... outburst, sounds to have had more the character of a sudden 'rush' than a gradual over-stimulation."

"And straight after half-time," noted Trevor. "What does that suggest to you? Anyone?"

"Done it himself during the break," muttered Ronny quietly.

"Yes. My thought, too," agreed the CEO. "My question is: how? Ron, Graeme, you're both supposed to be watching _our_ players. Jonny, you mind the exit, yes?"

"Jonah never left the changing room, I swear," declared Jonny.

Ronny was sweating. "Coach had me bailed up for a bit, talking tactics. I was playing out of position, remember, what with Solly being... gone, so I couldn't really argue with him."

"Quite fair, both of you. Graeme?"

"It wasn't _my_ fault! I had to try to look out for everyone! I was busy talking with Tiki, and I guess Jonah went out to the toilet."

"With a fix that he should never have brought into the room in the first place."

"I understand that, sir," said Ronny. "Jonah Latukefu is a smart guy, same as his brother."

"Mm. Yes, his brother. I want young Jonah brought to me, here, but I want Daniel to know nothing of it. He knows nothing about what we're doing, and I want it kept that way."

Ronny's brow furrowed. "Dan's a good footy player. He might be..."

Salmon interrupted. "He might indeed, in many ways. But he has something his brother lacks. Something lacked, indeed, by all of us here, in my estimation. Daniel Latukefu has a highly developed moral compass that is firmly fixed , as it were, on the side of the angels. We do not. Bring Jonah to me. Not now – I've an appointment to keep. I'm to identify the body of my dear brother, who has inexplicably washed up on one of the local beaches. I want Jonah here at a time that means he is not noticed, and not missed."

"What are you gonna do, boss?" asked Graeme.

"That will depend on him, and his behaviour," declared Trevor. "I hope he can continue to be useful, despite this curtailment of his playing career, for however long that lasts. I fear he's overstepped the boundaries of even <u>my</u> influence on the Disciplinary Tribunal. But he may be useful in other capacities. Perhaps help you with my sub-contractors, Jon?"

"I don't reckon I need much help. But if you've got plans of expansion, sure," the younger Lofton added hurriedly.

"Otherwise, I've got a few things I'd like to try out," suggested Darryl. "It's always useful to have a test subject."

Three other men at the table paled. Trevor Salmon wasn't one of them.

THERE WAS considerable surprise among the uniformed officers of Dunbar Police Station when it was realized that their two detectives were discussing Saturday's game at Tate Park. Even more startlingly, it was realized that <u>both</u> of them had actually been at the game!

Rita Mulholland was popular enough, sure, but nobody thought that she had any interest in footy. Quite the opposite, in fact. Yet there they were, deep in discussion of the match, the result, and even the rights and wrongs of some penalty decisions. None of them had been there themselves, so all shied away from getting involved in the conversation. Besides, the Detective Sergeant was clearly his usual irascible Monday morning self, despite the Demons' win.

Sterling had been as surprised as anyone when Rita told him she'd been in attendance, and promptly proved it by mentioning details that only a spectator could know. He accepted, and even faintly praised, her explanation: she'd been following up on the Tuafeulaki case. Running her eyes over the men she'd interviewed, hoping to get a better understanding of the character of some of them.

"Good move," he'd admitted. "Match day can bring out the best, and worst, in some blokes."

That led inevitably to discussion of Jonah Latukefu's send-off, and the apparent brain explosion which had led to it. Little that Sterling said varied much from what Rita had already heard from a few sources on Saturday. It had been extreme, but not entirely out of character. Jonah had always been something of a loose cannon. Yeah, he'd been getting noticeably worse this season.

"It's a pity that there's no drug testing carried out after games," she'd observed.

"The Club couldn't afford it!" Bob quickly replied, immediately on the defensive, but softened slightly with thought. "Never thought to need it, really, quiet little country club like ours. It's not like the boys are playing for sheep stations. The coach is the only one getting any sort of half-decent money, and even he's got a job on the side."

"It's volunteer work, I believe. As a carer," Rita said quietly.

"Yeah, well, some of those old buggers can be pretty generous to their 'carers', I believe."

The cold stare he got in response penetrated even his thick hide, and the conversation was quickly moved on.

"Like I said," the D. S. continued, "I know that sort of testing doesn't come cheap, and the Club's directors have never thought it a necessary expense."

"What about now, with what we know?"

"How do you mean?"

"The drug that was found in Solomona's body. What if it was performance enhancing?"

"Is there any evidence that it was?" Sterling asked cautiously.

"It's an unusual compound. I'm told that it's hard to know <u>what</u> all the effects might be. Doctor Cartwright's still working on it, but the sample size from Tuafeulaki's body wasn't as big as she'd prefer for experimenting. And that from Mike Salmon's body was even less helpful, beyond being able to identify it as the same."

"Call me if she does come up with anything useful. I suppose, at a pinch, with some evidence to back us up, we might be able to get some testing done ourselves, officially. If something warrants it."

"Something like another incidence of extreme behaviour?"

"If it's sufficiently out of character, yeah."

Even this reluctant concession was a big step for her boss, Rita realized. It was clear that he really did love, and was loyal to, his club. All the more reason then, for him to want to remove any stains on its character and reputation. But he couldn't, wouldn't, be rushed.

Rush? Oh damn, she was supposed to be in the morgue in a few minutes. It was mention of Mike Salmon's body that had jogged her usually reliable memory.

"I must dash! Better not keep Trevor Salmon waiting."

"No, better not do that," agreed the D. S. as she left hurriedly.

'Not a good man to annoy,' he thought to himself, rather uncomfortably.

IT WAS SLIGHTLY MORE than two hours after his meeting with his men, that Trevor Salmon arrived at the morgue. He was greeted by Doctor Cartwright and Detective Mulholland. Detective Sergeant Sterling avoided the morgue whenever possible, leery of both dead bodies and the coroner.

Maintaining a distance from Trevor also seemed a good idea at the moment. Mustn't risk 'compromising the investigation'.

When the sheet was withdrawn to reveal the sea-wracked face, Trevor inhaled deeply. He nodded, and said simply, "Yes. That's Michael. My brother."

Rita gestured surreptitiously to the doctor, who continued to pull back the sheet, revealing the dead man's ripped torso. There was no discernible reaction, and she discreetly signalled again for the covering to be replaced.

As Cartwright did so, Rita stopped herself from saying, "You're a cold fish, Mr. Salmon." Instead, she simply indicated that they should exit by the door they'd come in. The bereaved man showed no interest in lingering to pay his respects.

Back in the foyer she asked, "Any thoughts, or ideas, sir? That's how we found Michael's body."

Trevor shook his head. "If I had to guess, I'd say he went swimming when he was drunk, or stoned – he had some history of both. Got into trouble, drowned, and became fish food. Or got hit by a propeller of a passing boat – skipper probably wouldn't even have noticed the bump. I'm sorry, of course, but Michael has been his own worst enemy in many ways for a long time. This particular ending is surprising, I must admit, but his was a life that was never going to end well."

"Thank you, Mr. Salmon. Condolences for your loss, from D. S. Sterling too, of course."

"Mm. Do let me know if there's anything more that I can do for you, but I expect this to be a closed book now."

"Thank you, sir. Oh, I should mention, the coroner did find traces of drugs in your brother's body."

"Ah well, as I said, I'm not surprised. Poor old Michael. Always a silly fool."

Her face expressionless, Mulholland continued, "It seems to have been the same drug that was found in the body of Solomona Tuafeulaki. The young footballer who I spoke to you about recently. Remember?"

Not a flinch. "Really? How strange. You do hear stories of a drug problem in Dunbar, but somehow one expects it to be in... other parts of society. I really thought young – Tuafeulaki, wasn't it? I thought he was more sensible than that. I knew Michael wasn't always, but I can't imagine the two of them moving in the same circles. Mike was – artistic. Solomona was an earthier sort of bloke, as I recall. Keen on animals and football."

"That's my understanding, yes. No idea of any connection between them?"

"None at all, I'm afraid. If that's it, I'll be on my way."

"Of course. Thank you, Mr. Salmon, for your time, and your assistance."

"You're welcome, Detective. Good luck in your endeavours."

The pair shook hands, very formally, before Salmon left the foyer. Rita mused at his back as he went. 'The one obvious connection, of course, is you'.

Out in the street, Trevor was joined by Darryl Frankem, who'd been loitering under a tree for the whole time.

"How did it go?" asked the vet.

"Aggravating," was the blunt reply. "I expected it to be a formality. Identify the face, sign the appropriate paperwork, and that would be the end of it."

"Not so easy?"

"No. It turns out that there were still drug traces in Mike's body."

"Really? Wow..." There was a momentary frisson of pride in Frankem's voice, but he quickly moved on. "That's surprising after a long period of immersion in salt water. Er, any difficult questions?"

"Nothing that couldn't be sidestepped. Even when the police-woman mentioned that the same thing had been found in Solomona Tuafeulaki's body."

"That's not so good," said Frankem with concern.

Salmon shrugged casually. "There's nothing to connect them."

"As you say," Darryl replied quietly.

Both men stood in silent thought.

"What if a few random, totally unrelated deaths were to be discovered?" Darryl asked, his eyes scanning a little coterie of home-less folks in a park across the road.

"Mm. Might be useful. No. Better not give them any more samples to work from. Two deaths do not constitute a pattern. Mulholland may have her suspicions, but they'll find nothing. Her boss is inclined to be gung-ho, but he won't be looking hard. Not in our direction, especially. This will fade from view, and thought, soon enough."

"The proverbial 'too-hard' basket, eh?" said Frankem.

"I had one of those, back in my Public Service days," said an unexpected voice.

Engrossed in their own conversation, neither Frankem nor Salmon had noticed the approach of Cianawyn Lauder and Arthur Bayer. It was the latter who'd spoken, and now continued cheerily, "G'day Darryl! Pretty good rehearsal on Sunday, I thought."

"Oh! Yes – uh, hello. Hello, Arthur. Hello, Shan-win."

Cianawyn ignored the pronunciation, as usual, and smiled. "Hello, Darryl. Nice to see you."

"Yes, ah – this is my sometime employer, I've told you about him. Trevor Salmon – Shan-win Lauder and Arthur Bayer. They're involved in *Sweeney Todd* with me."

"Ah yes, your little artistic distraction. Pleasure to meet you both," said Trevor, suddenly the picture of geniality.

Handshakes were exchanged.

"Sorry, we can't stop to chat," explained Cianawyn. "We're expected in the morgue, of all places! Poor Arthur is expected to look at a body he found on a beach! I'm just here to hold his hand, in case he faints."

"Thank you, beloved," her husband replied through pursed lips.

"Just kidding, sweetheart," she answered merrily.

"Ri-i-ight," said her husband, drily. "Good to meet you, Trevor. See you tomorrow night at the theatre, Darryl."

Watching the two of them enter the morgue building, Trevor tapped a finger to his lips, thoughtfully.

"I thought I recognized him, the first time I met him at rehearsal. He's the bugger that Graeme and I met on the beach that time, when we found Mike's body."

"He hasn't recognized you?"

"It was wet, and he was distracted."

"Mm. Any prospect of a problem?"

"I wouldn't think so. Mind you, his wife does ask a lot of questions. A lot about Mike, now I think of it."

"Mm. I don't think I like that. Let's go, Darryl. We have a bit to think about ourselves."

.ooo.

21

———————

"Oh, this wretched terminal!" exclaimed Mary Fletcher.

"Bloody technology, eh?" chuckled the customer sympathetically. "Miss the old cash registers, eh?" he said.

She sighed, "I'm afraid I'd be fumbling that today, too. I can't seem to make my fingers work properly this morning, sorry, George."

"It's alright, Mary – hey, your hands really are trembling! Are you okay?"

"Oh! Oh, yes. Thanks, George. I'm just – we're just, a bit stressed."

"I'm sorry, Mary. Is there anything I can do?"

The shopkeeper stared, not at George but through him, for a long moment. "No. No, thank you, George," she finally said. "I'm sorry, I'm not sure what anyone can do. Certainly not Neil or I. Don't mind me. Here are your bits and pieces – have a nice day."

George took his hardware items, and said uncertainly, "Okay. Thanks, Mary. You take care of yourselves, you and Neil both."

Mary watched him go, through dull eyes. George was an old faithful customer, and she knew he was sincere. But her answer had been similarly sincere. The hardware store that she and her husband had both really enjoyed and appreciated, had suddenly become a burden.

They lived above the shop. It was the only substantial thing that they owned. It was also their sole source of income. All of their bills depended on its reliable regular takings.

She and Neil had spent long hours over the past two days, working out how long the business could sustain one or both of them being absent. In short, not very. A total closure, if both of them were away, could see problems in as little as two or three days, at worst. If either of them tried to operate single-handedly, they might manage a little more than a week.

Neither of the Fletchers were young. In truth, they'd already been considering selling up and retiring. It was never intended, or expected, that the hardware store would be passed down to their daughter. Their daughter. Georgie. Being taken advantage of, somewhere in Sydney. Yes, _somewhere_. That was the real problem.

There had been no contact from Georgie for months. The last address they'd written to had sent their card back marked 'RTS. Person unknown.' The mobile phone number that she'd had when she left, now gave only a 'disconnected' message from the service provider. Perhaps the phone had been lost, or stolen.

There may be a perfectly innocent explanation, but given what they now knew of their daughter's activities in Sydney, neither parent any longer considered such an option.

Damn the Salmon brothers! Damn them both to Hell!

THE FLETCHERS DIDN'T KNOW that if Hell was Mike Salmon's destination, he was already there.

Arthur Bayer knew, and he'd seen enough in the morgue to be sure that the departure for the afterlife hadn't been a pleasant one. He hadn't lingered very long over the corpse, just long enough to confirm that yes, this was the same body that he'd seen on Cemetery Beach. It had been in better condition then – all limbs intact, for one thing. But the washed-out face and hair looked about right. Most importantly, the great gash along the length of the body was exactly as had been etched in his memory.

"Do we know who he is? Was, rather?" he asked.

"I suppose it won't hurt for you to know," replied Detective Mulholland. She was mindful that Bayer and his wife had been helpful in the resolution of an earlier case, and she respected their thoughts. "This was Michael Salmon."

"Mike the breakfast deejay and sometime actor? Well, that explains why he hasn't been at the Terrence Theatre for a while!"

"Sorry – where?"

"Dunbar District Players. He was supposed to be playing the lead there in *Sweeney Todd*. Caused quite some chaos when he went AWOL."

"I knew nothing about this connection," Rita admitted.

"There's no reason why you would, I suppose," said Arthur. "Nobody in the theatre knew anything other than that he'd taken off without a word. Surprising, but not entirely out of character, from what I gather. I never met the man – I got drafted in as a replacement after he vanished. There was no reason for anyone to suspect Foul Play. I guess it was assumed that, if there were any real concerns, the family would be the ones to talk to the police."

"Hmm. His family consists entirely of his brother Trevor, it seems."

"Ah, that explains how he came to be on the footpath outside. We just bumped into him on our way in. I'd never met him before, but he happened to be with another member of our cast."

"Really? Who?"

"Darryl Frankem. He's a vet. Works with Trevor's greyhounds, I understand."

"Interesting. I'd better look into the theatre crowd," said Rita. "We've no other leads to go on, apart from the radio station, and I'd intended to talk to the people there as soon as possible."

"Well, if you're going to talk to the Players, you'd better start with the director, Shauna Shallacot. She's been with them quite a while. Knew Mike of old. Cianawyn's got her number."

"Oh? Is Ms Lauder involved with the Players too?"

"Wardrobe mistress. Sees and hears a lot."

"I can imagine," said the detective shrewdly. "I think I should talk with your wife."

"Good idea. She'll be more use to you than I am. She's right outside."

And so it was that the two women spent some productive time conversing in the morgue's anteroom. Cianawyn now had an interested ear (besides those of her husband and her mother) into which she could convey her thoughts, observations, and suspicions. Rita rapidly filled several pages of her notebook. Names, observations – both Cianawyn's and her own, in the shorthand-like code that only she could decipher.

Once satisfied, she thanked the couple for their willing assistance, and made her way back to the station for more paperwork, and a likely long talk with D. S. Sterling.

Cianawyn and Arthur, for their part, both felt a very strong need for coffee. They went to the Flying Saucer, Arthur's current favourite.

They'd scarcely had their coffees and croissants delivered by Naomi, Gordon Teller's regular object of desire, when that very man himself walked into the café. As he crossed paths with Naomi, he gave her arm an affectionate squeeze, which provoked only an answering smile.

"Greetings, my favourite couple!" boomed the announcer.

It was as if, having not long come out of the studio, he was over-compensating for having had to moderate his voice for hours. Unbidden, but not unwelcome, he joined them at their table.

"Did you have a good shift?" asked Cianawyn.

"As entertaining as ever. I was, anyway. A couple of callers on the 'What's That Sound?' competition were less so. Some people just don't like to be told they're wrong."

"Very true," agreed Arthur, not mentioning that Teller was sometimes one of those people.

"I'd be doing away with the competition, if I had my way," stated Gordon. "I think it's past its use-by date. Some of the things that have been recorded are unfairly obscure, in my humble opinion. But it's an old favourite of Mike's, so for now, it stays."

The couple exchanged looks. Cianawyn shrugged and said, "It's not like we were sworn to secrecy, hon. Rita said she'd be following up very soon, anyway."

"Fair enough," agreed her husband. "A bit of news for you, Gordo. You won't have to worry about Mike Salmon taking his shift back."

"Eh?"

"His body was found washed up on one of the local beaches," Arthur explained.

"Oh. Well, that's good to know. From a purely selfish point of view. I didn't mean to sound insensitive. Shame for poor old Mike that he drowned, of course..."

"He didn't drown." Cianawyn interrupted his casual observations. "He was murdered."

"Oh." Gordon paused. "That's different. Poor old bugger." Another pause. "How do you know?"

"We're just back from the morgue. It was Arthur who first found the body, and he had to confirm that its condition was as he'd seen it."

Now Gordon was genuinely derailed. "Condition? That sounds... messy. Unpleasant," he said, now quiet.

"It was," agreed Arthur, declining to go into detail.

To his credit, Gordon didn't ask. Instead, he said, "I thought you both seemed a bit quieter than usual. My apologies." If he wasn't sincere, he was a fine actor.

Cianawyn continued the update. "We've heard that someone from the police will be visiting CRD-FM soon. Routine questions, I assume. How well was Mike known, any enemies, the usual stuff."

"They'll have to start with Old Glory, the Station Manager, I suppose. Or Desley Hattersley. The Mad Hatter's been there longer than anybody, doing publicity. Most of the other office staff are pretty new," said Gordon.

"What about all the on-air people? Do you have much to do with each other?" Cianawyn asked, correctly anticipating one of Rita's questions.

Teller shrugged. "Some do, some don't. The old hands have known each other for a long time. We don't socialize, though. To be honest, Fitzroy, Mike and I haven't gotten on very well for years."

'Too much competing ego', Lauder surmised accurately.

"Some of the younger crew spend some time with Mike or me. Spent, obviously, in his case. He saw himself as a mentor. Voice of experience, that sort of thing, y'know. Me, I'm just interested in whether somebody's good company. Like you two are. Like I try to be."

"That sounds more than fair, old mate," said Arthur.

It was clear that the news had affected Gordon, however much he tried not to show it. Uncharacteristically, he was the first to leave, after downing his coffee in a few gulps. Normally he'd savour the brew while holding court, but not today. He gave Arthur a mate-y pat on the shoulder, and kissed Cianawyn's hand in the courtly manner he'd seen her husband use.

"See you soon, good people," he said, departing much more quietly than he'd arrived.

Even Naomi received a farewell that was much less demonstrative than usual, to her surprise and possibly disappointment.

"He's more disturbed than he's letting on," said Arthur.

"I thought so, too. I wonder – was it the news of Mike's murder, or the prospect of a police interview?"

Sometimes, Cianawyn found it hard not to be cynical.

.ooo.

22

In the quiet of her room in Cromwell House, Cailleach Steele found it easy to think. There wasn't the interruption of other residents wanting 'a little chat'. Or they'd insist that the television be on in the Common Room, for tedious daytime soap operas, inane chat shows, or movies that she hadn't enjoyed any of the first six times that she'd sat through them.

In her own room, the TV could be left off, and her radio tuned to a station playing only classical music, and kept at an audible but not intrusive volume. The curtains were drawn, and the only light was that of her bed lamp, which she'd dimmed to half intensity.

Callie sat in her comfortable armchair, hands clasped lightly across her tummy.

The girl who'd come in to offer morning tea had almost slipped away quietly again, thinking that the old woman was asleep. Unexpectedly, though, the request was made: "A black tea with no sugar, please. And a little cake if you have it. Thank you."

The girl was sure the woman's head hadn't moved.

"Certainly, Mrs. Steele," she'd said.

Now, a half hour later, only a few crumbs remained on the paper plate. The cup was still one third full, but the temperature of its contents had fallen below what was appealing. Black tea, Callie had found, was excellent food for thought. Hummingbird cake, though, was even better.

The current subject of deep contemplation was the conversation that she'd had with her darling daughter on Sunday afternoon. Cian had related in detail the news about the Fletchers.

A terrible thing, both women had agreed. While they would wish it otherwise, both understood that there seemed little prospect of either distressed parent travelling to Sydney to search for their missing daughter. All that any of them could do was fret.

Cailleach was not the fretting type. No known address, or phone number, but there <u>must</u> be a way to locate Georgie. She didn't believe that the girl was dead. That wasn't blind optimism. Gaelic tradition put a lot of store by maternal intuition. If Georgie had died, her mother would know, at some deep, primal level. Callie was sure of that.

So, she must be somewhere. Perhaps she had moved on from Sydney, but it was a place to start. The biggest place in the country, unfortunately.

What else was known? She'd worked, at least once, as an actress. Not the sort of movie that one approved of, but every movie, whatever the type, required a cast. And that cast had to come from somewhere.

A student of human nature, Callie reasoned that anyone willing to appear in a blue movie would be driven by a strong desire to perform. They would probably want a bigger, more 'mainstream' audience to show off their talents to.

She reached into the cupboard beside her chair, and drew out her trusty laptop computer. It wasn't the latest model. No need for the latest bells and whistles. It wasn't used often, these days, but it was always kept charged in case of an emergency, such as extreme boredom.

After a wait, Dunbar's internet speed being notoriously slow, she typed 'Talent Agencies – Sydney' into her search engine. The resulting list was distressingly long. Ce la vie. What else did she have? Cian had mentioned the last known address, or at least the suburb. Callie had lived and worked in Sydney as a journalist for a long time in her younger years, and she still knew her way around.

She scanned the list carefully. Any address that was within reasonable range of that suburb, especially for a young woman without a car, was regarded as potentially promising. She copied the name of any such agency, together with its contact details, and entered them into a spreadsheet she created.

If she had no success with this list, she'd extend the search to other postcodes. She finished with over twenty-five agency names. Still a challenge, but she hadn't expected this to be easy.

What next? She wanted to get in touch with each agency. Find out if Georgie Fletcher was on anyone's books. But how should she approach this?

An elderly woman randomly telephoning to ask about one of their girls would sound, at the very least, peculiar. If it was an agency with any substantial ties to the pornography industry, it would probably sound suspicious. Must do better. An email would be better.

Casting her mind back to her days as a journalist, she recalled that talent agencies, casting agents, and producers usually communicated through their own professional networks. Nowadays such networks were almost certainly on-line, whereas once they'd been contained in an assortment of 'little black books' across the industry.

That meant her excuse – her 'cover story' – had to be carefully crafted.

A polite knock on her door heralded lunch. Good. Not that she was very hungry, and the pasta dish that was today's special did nothing to excite her. But another black tea would be very welcome, thank you. Any more of that Hummingbird cake? That's a shame. A small citrus tart would be lovely, thank you.

When the lunch plates were taken away, there was a scant mouthful missing from the pasta. The tea cup was empty, and the cake plate didn't have so much as a crumb on it. This time, however, Mrs. Steele really was sleeping.

It was only a light nap, though, and it enabled Callie's subconscious to get to work on the problem. When she awoke, less than an hour later, she had a clear picture in mind of the email which would be sent to each talent agency.

Dear -----------

I have been engaged by one of our local volunteer groups here in Dunbar to help produce a promotional video. Their aim is to profile their work, training and supporting young people in our region of the Coast.

One of the media identities here, Mr. Michael Salmon, recommended a particular actress as potentially suitable to us. She is a local girl named Georgie Fletcher, who now resides in Sydney. I understand she may be using a professional name now, but I am sure her agent would know both.

Unfortunately, Mr. Salmon had lost contact with Ms Fletcher some time ago. He himself has recently left Dunbar, so I am unable to obtain any further details.

I realise that I am being optimistic, but having received such positive reports of Ms Fletcher's suitability, I feel obliged to at least try.

Are you, by any chance, representing her, or perhaps you can direct me to who is?

She is an attractive brunette in her late teens, although she can readily pass for older. 174 centimetres tall, with a good figure and a lightly tanned complexion.

If you are able to assist, please contact me at this email address. My sincere thanks, on behalf of both myself and the dedicated volunteers whom I am assisting.

Yours sincerely, C. Steele. Dunbar.

'That's satisfactory,' she thought, as she added her phone number. 'Polite, neutral, professional but not too much so. Tells quite a reasonable story. It shouldn't hurt to name-drop Mr. Salmon, since he and his brother were responsible for getting the poor girl to Sydney in the first place. If anything that they said was true, the name may actually have some cachet in the industry. Right, let's run it up the flagpole and see who salutes.'

Twenty-seven cut-and-pastes later, all of the emails were sent.

"Who knows?" Callie said to her radio, which was still quietly producing the soundtrack to her efforts. "It's better than doing nothing, and it might just work."

.ooo.

23

———————

As many people had observed, Ted Beaumaris was 'a good kid'. Not the brightest young spark in Dunbar, but not stupid. He worked hard, and loved his parents.

He'd been beyond thrilled to receive his own car. Okay, a 2010 model Commodore wasn't exactly flash, but it was bright red, clean, had a decent 6-cylinder engine, good steering and brakes, and most importantly of all, it was <u>his</u>!

He deeply appreciated his parents' generosity. Ted knew, too, that the gift was in recognition of how well he was doing at work. To go from a labourer to a proper apprentice was more than he'd really expected, however much effort he'd willingly put in.

His supervisor, Jonny, had been really supportive. He'd really encouraged Ted, and when he'd seen how keen the young bloke was to keep doing better, he'd even come up with a way to help.

'Supplements', Jonny had called them, and they really did make a difference. Tasks that had seemed too hard before, now came easily to him. Or if they didn't, he wasn't so intimidated by their difficulty, and he found a way to persevere, usually successfully.

It had been an early start on site this morning, and the whole team, Ted included, had got their work done quickly and well. When the clouds rolled in threateningly in the middle of the afternoon, Jonny Lofton was content to let everyone leave early.

"Busy day tomorrow, but," he warned them all. To a very select few he added, "Here's a little something that'll help. Careful with it, mind." Ted was one of those few.

Very glad to be home earlier than usual, the Beaumaris' pride and joy was happy to help his Mum with chores.

Preparing the dinner, Laura suddenly exclaimed, "Blast! I need some potatoes! These have gone to seed."

"I'll go get them for you, Mum."

"Hmm – thanks, son, but I'd rather select them myself. There are a few different types of potato, that cook better in different ways. I'd like to see what's available."

"Okay. I can drive you to the shops."

Laura smiled. Ted was so obviously keen to take her out in his new car. "Alright, son. Thanks, that would be lovely. Er, you might change out of your work clothes first?"

"Oh, sure."

A few minutes later, the young man was in his bedroom. He'd stood in a small cloud of spray-on deodorant, and changed into jeans and a clean t-shirt. He yawned. A great, jaw-cracking yawn.

'Jeez! I didn't realize I was that tired,' he thought to himself. 'Can't let Mum down, but.'

He reached for his work pants, now folded on the floor. From a button-down pocket he took Jonny's "little something".

"This oughta keep me awake," he said to himself.

It wasn't a great distance from the Beaumaris' home to the small shopping centre. Laura didn't take long to select her potatoes, and a few other vegetables that she suddenly fancied. She took the time to explain to Ted why she made the choices that she did. One day, she reasoned, he'll be cooking and shopping for himself. Better he knows these things.

Her son was happy for the domestic education. Inordinately happy, Laura thought briefly. 'Oh well, with the new car, he's probably giving more thought to his own independence.'

Ted's effervescent good humour was only increasing as he left the car park for the short drive home.

"Gosh, this is a good car," he told his mother excitedly. "Got a lot more grunt than you'd expect, and handles really, really well. Watch this..."

Laura screamed as the shiny red Commodore skidded, out of control, around a bend.

Ted Beaumaris had his eyes closed, and didn't even see the tree that killed them both.

.ooo.

24

———————

At breakfast in the Common Room, Callie heard about the car accident on the CRD-FM morning program. Not on the news – that was a nationally franchised bulletin. Very little that happened in Dunbar was deemed important enough to get air time.

But Gordon Teller took an interest in his community. When someone had told him the night before about the tragic loss that had befallen a popular local teacher, he wanted it to be known. Not naming any names, he simply explained that there'd been a terrible incident involving a car, and the family of a teacher, and offered his sincere condolences.

A cold chill went down the spines of both Cianawyn and Arthur when they heard the broadcast. Although childless, they'd befriended a few teachers and students through the Players, and hoped that it was nobody they knew. Somehow, though, Cianawyn's intuition told her otherwise.

A similar frisson afflicted her mother. Abruptly she lost interest in her breakfast. "I think I'll go back to my room," she announced, standing up suddenly. "I'll just get a cup of tea from the kitchen."

"Are you alright?" asked Kenneth Derbishire, one of her table-mates. "Here, let me help you."

Even clutching her trusty 'wheelie walker', Callie was clearly unsteady on her feet. Ordinarily she'd have waved away an offer of assistance, even from someone she liked. But the flash of inspiration had un-nerved her, hence the momentary difficulty with balance.

Leaning as gently and unobtrusively as she could on Kenneth's proffered arm, she made her way to the kitchen and ordered her 'thinking brew'. It wasn't hot enough to be a 'scald risk' – that was a Cromwell House rule – but a thin wisp of steam did rise from the plastic mug.

"I'll take that," said the retired policeman, gently but firmly.

"Thank you, Kenneth," Callie said, quietly grateful for the help, as they made their way carefully to her room.

"Sitting down, or lying down?" he asked solicitously.

"Sitting, thank you. I think better that way."

Derbishire helped her to the armchair, and placed the tea on the convenient side table.

"Feeling better?" he asked.

"Somewhat, yes. I do apologize for taking you away from your breakfast."

"That's fine. I was pretty much finished, anyway. Just enjoying the company. Can I ask, what upset you? Was it that story about the car crash?"

"Yes, it was. Silly, really. It's not like there were any details. I just had the sudden feeling that... it's hard to explain... it felt somehow... close to home."

"Cian and Arthur aren't teachers, are they? Didn't used to be?"

"No. Nothing like that. It was just – a feeling."

"One you need to think about?" Kenneth ventured.

"I'd rather not, to be honest, but I'm sure I will. I'll find something to distract myself. Keep my mind occupied."

"If you're sure you're alright now?"

"Yes, thank you. Sorry to be a nuisance."

"You weren't, at all. Should I get the staff to check in on you?"

"They will soon enough, anyway. I'll be fine."

Both of them smiling, Derbishire waved as he departed, closing the door behind him. Callie looked at the door for a few moments, then leaned back in her chair. She didn't like being unsettled like this. It was as she'd told Kenneth – she needed distracting.

She switched on the radio. The classical station, as usual. A baroque piece, ideal. Mozart, she recognized. Several minutes of good music in a room with muted light wasn't enough, though. She still felt troubled, but helpless about that particular matter.

Should she call darling Cianawyn? No, better not. If the issue <u>was</u> there, and she couldn't see how, it would likely only add to the distress, for both of them.

With a decisive squaring of her shoulders, she pulled out her laptop. She went straight to the Inbox of her email account. Ah – that was good! There were eleven replies to 'C. Steele – Dunbar' from different talent agencies. With an effort, she contained her eagerness and optimism.

The first five offered nothing. The person who'd written the sixth reply remembered interviewing someone answering Ms Fletcher's description. He remembered her Dunbar origin, being an old Coast resident himself. But no, they specialized in singers and dancers, and she'd had no confidence as either. They hadn't even kept her details.

'Still,' thought Callie, 'I believe I'm on the right track.'

Three more negative responses. Then, the second-last email to have arrived was promising. Yes, they sometimes got referrals from Mr. Salmon (though they didn't specify which one). Yes, they had a record on file of a Miss Fletcher coming in for an interview. No, they hadn't taken her on as a client. They were principally a modelling agency, with a handful of high-profile actors. Miss Fletcher at that point hadn't been interested in modelling, and wasn't a known quantity as a performer. They'd referred her to another agency who specialized in 'Extras', and 'talent' to take on small roles in film and television.

Alas, Callie realized, that particular agency – 'HighTide' – wasn't the other one to have replied to her.

"Not yet, anyway," she told herself firmly.

Closing the laptop and laying it on the bed, she leaned back in her chair. She closed her eyes, enjoying Mozart and thinking positive thoughts.

An hour and a half later, she was woken by today's Room Service attendant, a jovial Tongan woman who wasn't especially attentive to whether or not residents were asleep when she came into their room.

"Morning tea!" she'd shouted cheerfully as she entered.

Callie sat up sharply. "I'm not asleep! Just resting my eyes!"

"O' course you were, darlin'. You want tea or coffee?"

A couple of blinks, and a little shake of the head later, the reply came." "Tea, please. Black, with no sugar."

"Gotcha. You wanna biscuit? Or a lamington?"

"Not one of those with the awful fake cream in the middle?"

"Nah, these are plain. Helped make 'em myself," the woman replied with a grin that stood out in the semi-darkness.

"One of those would be very pleasant, then. Thank you."

The morning tea was promptly delivered. Soon refreshed, Callie opened her laptop again. Three more replies in her Inbox. The last of them from HighTide Talent.

Diligently, she checked the other two first, just in case. She needn't have bothered, but better to be sure.

The reply she wanted was from Anthony Silver, the head of High-Tide. He thanked Mr. or Ms Steele (she'd deliberately left it uncertain) for their correspondence. He confirmed that yes, Georgie Fletcher was one of his clients. She was working under the name 'Gigi Sands' now, a discreet homage to her coastal origins, of which she was still proud. Thus, he was sure she would be interested in the proposed project.

He was very pleased on her behalf. She was a natural talent, he said, and would undoubtedly make the most of the opportunity. He couldn't answer on her behalf, but given the circumstances, had forwarded the details to her. He'd strongly recommended that she reply herself regarding her decision, and to discuss dates and times, travel, accommodation if required. On the matter of her availability, though, he cautioned that the young lady had landed a significant stage role which may affect the timing of the project.

He also mentioned the relevant minimum award rate she should expect to be paid, and politely pointed out that, as her agent, such payment would be expected to go through him. As Mr./Ms Steele had made the initial approach, and, given the unorthodox circumstances, he'd be happy to reduce his commission down to 7.5%.

Callie wasn't sure, but she thought that this was genuinely a good discount. Anthony Silver seemed to be a nice man, she thought. That notion was reinforced in the next paragraph, when he noted that for Ms Fletcher's security, he could not provide any direct contact details for her. Any decision to correspond further must be up to the performer herself. He hoped sincerely that she would do so, as the experience and the exposure would surely benefit her career.

'I wonder if he knows what type of exposure she's already experienced in her career?' pondered Callie.

Judging by the tone of his email, she suspected not. She guessed Silver was a father himself, and genuinely protective of his Talent.

"I wish you and your group every success. I hope that I've been able to help. Yours sincerely, Anthony Silver," she read aloud. "Well, Mr. Silver, you have, to the best of your ability. Now it's up to the lass herself."

She snapped the laptop shut, and hauled herself up from the chair. A few coins were taken from the top drawer of the bedside table, and the 'wheelie walker' firmly grasped. Her balance still wasn't quite 100%, she'd realized as she stood.

"But I _am_ feeling very much better," she told herself.

A cappuccino from the machine in the Common Room was very much in order. If Kenneth Derbishire was there, she'd be happy to buy him one too, as a thank you for his courtesy and care. She might just share this news with him, too.

Just as she was halfway out the door, her mobile phone rang, vibrating against the top of her bedside table where she'd left it to charge. The first impulse was to ignore it and go for the coffee. But what if it was Cian, or someone else important? Well, nobody else was that important really. Arthur was close. Still, one never knew.

Cailleach wasn't able to dash across the room, so inevitably the phone had rung off by the time she got to it. She checked the call register. No, it hadn't been her darling daughter. She didn't recognize the number. There had been a voice message left, though. Again, the impulse was to get coffee first, and check the phone later.

As she stood looking at the device, though, she felt a clear premonition that this was important. She played the voice message.

"Hello, Mr. Steele's office? This is Gigi – Georgie Fletcher. I'm interested in the video you're making. I... I would like to come back to Dunbar, at least for a visit. I'm rehearsing for a play at the Arcadium, but I think I could be spared for a few days, if that's okay? I – er – might need some help with transport. I don't have a lot of money to spend at the moment... I _am_ interested though. Here's my number..."

Callie wrote it down, feeling positive. It was a hoax on her own part, and she'd have to let the girl down gently, but it was reassuring that she'd expressed a willingness to come back to Dunbar, even temporarily. She hadn't burned her bridges, then.

And the news of impending stage work was a huge relief. The Arcadium was a prestigious old theatre. It didn't specialize in musicals, or big-name celebrity vehicles, like some did. It was more usually home to more classical plays, or new ones in a similar style. Surely that suggested that she'd been able to move on from a more unsavoury type of performance.

Her hand hovered over the phone. To call, or not to call? Right now, that is. Would it seem too eager if she returned the call immediately?

Wait – what was she thinking? She wasn't going to _hire_ Georgie. There _was_ no promotional video. For a moment, Callie had been caught up in her own fiction. No, what mattered was the contact. To talk to the girl, and try to ascertain that she was safe and well. She did sound that way, which was an encouraging start. Although she had mentioned that money was tight.

No. Prevaricating was pointless. She sat in her armchair, a pad and pen at the ready. Be positive. Make the call.

The phone at the other end was answered almost immediately.

"Gigi Sands – hello?"

"Miss Fletcher?"

There was a momentary pause, then a cautious, "Yes."

"Good morning. My name is Cailleach Steele. I've just received your message."

"Oh! Ms Steele! I'm sorry – your voice surprised me. I expected... er..."

"Someone male, and probably younger?"

"Well, um, yes. I'm sorry."

"Quite alright. I'm sorry to disappoint you."

"Oh, no! It's just that... sorry..."

"Please stop apologizing, Miss Fletcher. It's I who must apologize to you, for another disappointment."

"The project is off? You've found another actress."

"No. There is, in fact, no project. There never was. Wait – please listen. My name is Cailleach Steele, and I am in Dunbar. I'm calling you because there are some people here who are very concerned about you."

There was a silence, long enough for Callie to fear she'd been hung up on.

Then a quiet voice asked, "You mean my parents?"

"Yes, among others."

Another silence.

"Are you a private investigator or something?"

The short laugh couldn't be held in. "Hardly! I'm an elderly widow, who is trying to reassure some worried people. And to help a young lady far from home, if it's wanted and needed and in any way possible for me to accomplish."

"You're a friend of my Mum and Dad?"

"Not directly. My daughter works in the same theatre group that you used to. Where your parents did until very recently."

"Oh my God! Please tell her, <u>please</u>, to be really careful of Mike Salmon!"

"Oh?" responded Callie, as neutral as possible.

"He was the one that got me to come to Sydney in the first place. Did you know that?"

"I've heard something to that effect. The promise of a big career?"

Georgie took a deep breath.

Cailleach shared with her daughter Cianawyn an apparently mutant gift that prompted people to tell them their life stories. Usually unrequested, and often from folks who were almost complete strangers. Now, young Miss Fletcher had fallen under the same spell.

"It wasn't just that," she said. "Tell your daughter, never, ever accept anything from Mike!"

"Gifts, you mean?"

"No, pills. Something to cheer her up. That's how he described them to me. And they worked, too. All my frustrations about being stuck in boring Dunbar, well, they didn't quite go away, but they didn't matter so much. And he <u>gave</u> them to me. Free. Not many, but enough. He did warn me that when I got to Sydney, I'd have to pay for them. But he told me where to go for the best deal, if I needed them."

"And did you?"

"Before long, yeah. The doors Mike said would open for me stayed shut. I got a bit of work in a supermarket, just enough to rent a lousy little room. But I felt awful. Frustrated. So, I followed up on one of his contacts. One of Trevor's, actually. Trevor is Mike's brother."

"I've heard of him."

"He's a lot sharper than Mike. Not in a good way. This mate of Trevor's – a business associate, he called himself, was helpful up to a very certain point. Yes, he could get me Major Happy…"

"Sorry, who?"

"Major Happy. That's what the pills are called."

"Clever name. It sounds quite harmless."

"Yeah, it does, doesn't it? It gets a hook in you. You don't need more and more, you just need <u>it</u>. And it cost more than a part-time checkout girl could afford."

"I see. The frustration increases, and the desire for this Major Happy does too."

"That's it. You understand, Ms Steele. Then, this business associate of Trevor's has a suggestion of how I could make some money. 'You're an actress, I hear,' he says. 'I could find work for you. Not too difficult. Pays alright. Enough to help you along,' he says."

"I can guess," said Callie. "I know what sort of work he meant. The sort of movies he had in mind."

"Not movies plural. Not for me. Just one. I only ever did one. How did you –"

"It's how I came to be looking for you, my dear. Unfortunately, your father saw the movie in question."

"Oh no – God, no..."

There was a much longer silence this time. "How is he?" the girl asked.

"Upset. Confused. Angry – not at you!" Callie hurried to reassure. "His only thought of you is worry. Concern that you're alright, not... abused, or in... any other sort of trouble."

"I'm not now. It was a close thing, but I lucked out. One of the other girls in the movie, Ophelia – it really is her real name. Mad, isn't it? Ophelia and I just clicked right away, and she's really helped. Looked after me. She's got a nice apartment in Neutral Bay, and she let me move into her second bedroom."

"This girl sounds... well-equipped, for someone working in a pornographic film," said Callie dubiously.

"She's done a lot of them, and the income is good if you get paid in money, not drugs. Ophelia says she really enjoys the work. Getting paid is a bonus, she reckons, though I don't think that's quite true. She does say, though, that she has a better choice of partners than if she was a hooker."

Very glad that her blush wasn't visible over the phone, Callie managed to stammer, "You're not...?"

"God, no! I've never been <u>that</u> desperate for money! And Ophelia's really helped me with getting off Major Happy. She had her own addiction issues a while back, that she managed to kick. I reckon that's why she took me under her wing, y'know. She just works in the business now because she likes it, and it pays pretty well. Me, I want to be a <u>real</u> actress."

"That one film may come back to haunt you, you realize?"

"You know what they say about showbiz. Any publicity is good publicity. It's not like I used my own name. Not even Gigi Sands. It was something like 'Stormy Coast' or 'Stormy Weather', I think. If, when I'm famous, someone thinks they recognize me, I can be flattered or outraged, depending on how I feel."

"I can't fault your confidence," the old woman admitted. "What about your parents, though? You've made no effort to contact them."

There was another silence. Had she pushed too hard?

The voice was quiet again. "I was ashamed," Georgie admitted. "Firstly, because I'd run out of money so quickly, when I'd been so sure of myself. Nobody likes to admit they've made a mistake."

"Yet, we all do, my dear. The trick is to learn from them, not keep making them in different guises."

"I understand, I think. Anyway, after that movie, it was another sort of shame. I just didn't know what to say to them. How to answer any questions they might ask. I'm not a very good liar."

'A strange admission from an actor,' was Callie's silent thought. Aloud she said, "You've been honest with me. You can be honest with them. Perhaps spare some details, but things are looking up, aren't they? I understand you're working at the Arcadium. That's a feather in any young performer's cap."

The smile on Georgie's face was almost audible over the phone. "Yeah! I'm in a revamped version of an old Roman age comedy. 'Diskolos', it means 'the grumpy old man'. I haven't got a principal role, but I'm not stuck in the chorus, either. I've got a few parts. Plenty of lines, and lots of stage time."

"That's wonderful. I'm glad you're excited. I'm sure your parents will be, too, if you'll allow me to tell them. I'd like to tell them a little more. Nothing too specific. That you're alive, and things are going well after a difficult start, let's say."

"That... sounds good."

"Georgie, if I 'prime' them for you, will you please call them your-self? Let them hear your voice? As a mother myself, I know how much that means."

"I will. Thanks. And, hey, thinking of your daughter – remember what I said about Mike Salmon. He's trouble."

"I do appreciate the warning, dear girl. Thank you. Mike Salmon has... parted ways with the Dunbar Players. I don't think that he will be causing any trouble for anyone."

"That's good. That's really, really good. Thank you for finding me and getting in touch, Mrs. Steele. I really did need that, even if I wasn't admitting it to myself."

"Don't be too hard on yourself, lass. That's a trap that many of us have fallen into over the years."

"Talking of traps, if Mike's gone, watch out for Trevor. He's prob-ably worse. Tell your daughter to watch out."

"I will, thank you. I'll call you soon, if that's alright. After I've contacted your parents."

"Yeah. Yeah. That... that'll be good. Thanks again, Mrs. Steele."

As the phone went silent, Callie closed her eyes and tilted her head back. The road hadn't always been easy between her and Cianawyn. Not for either of them, if she was really honest with herself. But there were so many ways in which it could have been so much worse. It didn't hurt to be reminded of that.

She would call the Fletchers, and share the gist of what she hoped would be comforting news. First, though, she would call her own darling daughter, and pass on Georgie's news. It fitted with her own forebodings about the property developer, as well as Cianawyn's own misgivings.

And <u>then</u>, she would reward herself with coffee.

.ooo.

25

———————

The coroner's report on the fatal car accident didn't take long to prepare. It was succinct. Death had been nearly instantaneous for both victims. Severe impact trauma to both passenger and driver. That much was straightforward.

Sadly, Doctor Cartwright had another fact to reveal. Examination of the young driver's body clearly indicated the presence of a drug that almost certainly was responsible for his apparent loss of control of the car.

It was the same drug that had been found in the bodies of Solomona Tuafeulaki and Mike Salmon. This time, the concentration was higher.

THE LUNCHTIME SHIFT at Community Radio Dunbar-FM was being covered by one of the station's 'fill-in' announcers. He was an earnest young man, but with a voice too monotone for a career in broadcasting. However, he knew which buttons to push, and he could read an advertisement or a community announcement quite capably.

All of the regular staff, on-air and office personnel, were squeezed into the boardroom for an Urgent Meeting. The station manager, Gloria Barnet, was holding court, as she preferred.

"The police will be arriving later this afternoon to commence interviewing everyone. I have prepared a roster, which I'll distribute to everyone shortly. We are advised that these interviews are routine procedure, as all of you were acquainted with Mike Salmon, and I see no reason to doubt that assurance. I find it impossible to conceive that anyone here could have been involved in his death..."

A few looks were exchanged around the room. Clearly a few people had better imaginations than the station manager.

"However," she continued, "I believe it's possible that someone may know some small details of Mike's personal life or activities, which could shed some light on this terrible situation. So, please, everyone, do apply some thought to it , and offer any information that you can."

There were general murmurs of agreement around the room.

"Now, to address the pertinent question for CRD-FM, what should be said publicly? How much information should we give?"

"Gordon, you lifted the lid on that car accident. I imagine you can't wait to 'scoop' this story either," said Fitzroy Carlton peevishly.

Breaking local stories should be his bailiwick, as the announcer of longest standing, or so the veteran believed. Teller's reply was simple and to the point.

"Pull your head in, Fitz."

"Now, now, gentlemen," Gloria interposed quickly. "While Gordon did act without authorization, we have spoken subsequently, and I accept that his reasoning was sound. The breakfast program is our highest rating timeslot, and the Beaumaris family are well known, in the school community especially. He didn't name anyone, but I agree that he's probably headed off some speculation and even gossip within that community."

To Gordon's surprise, Angelika Judd also came to his defence. "I think that by saying as much as he did, Gordon at least allayed the concerns of some listeners who'd had no idea of who was involved in the incident that had so many emergency vehicles dashing along the main road. Saying that it was the family of a teacher eliminated a lot of possibilities. That would have been reassuring to plenty."

"Hmph," grumbled Carlton.

"Back to the matter at hand," said 'Old Glory', firmly reasserting control. "What, if anything, is to be said about poor Mike?"

"Huh – 'poor Mike' probably had it coming," said Gwen Hardy bitterly.

That surprised most in the room. The receptionist was thought of as the sweetest and mildest of girls.

"I'm sorry," she continued, "but he could be a real old lecher sometimes, and I hated that."

A few sidelong glances were directed at Gordon, all of which he studiously ignored.

Angelika folded her arms. "Gwen's right, I'm afraid. He was the same at the theatre."

Gloria looked stunned. "Why wasn't I told any of this?" she demanded.

"I did try, but you told me I was 'misinterpreting' him," said Gwen. "Told me he was just being friendly."

Gordon bit his tongue to avoid telling Old Glory that she'd have forgiven 'good old Mike' anything this side of statutory rape, and that Desley Hattersley was worse.

Indeed, it was the 'Mad Hatter' who spoke next. "Well, I've certainly not heard anything of this. Mike was always a perfect gentleman."

"Yes, you have, and no, he wasn't," snapped Lucy Miles, another part-time producer and occasional office assistant, who was also inclined to be quiet and un-noticed. "I complained to you months ago that he'd been saying some inappropriate things to me. You told me I was being silly. Just about accused me of making it up, and that Mister Salmon was not that kind of a man."

"I have no recollection of that at all," said Desley sniffily. "I remember you making that sort of complaint about Gordon Teller."

"Yes, I did, and you jumped on him real quick," Lucy confirmed.

"Too bloody right," agreed Gordon, just under his breath.

Young Lucy continued. "And Gordon came and apologized to me. Said he'd never meant to offend me or upset me. No such thing from Mike Salmon, though, even if you ever <u>did</u> say anything to him!"

Desley dabbed at her eyes with a tissue. She'd held an unreciprocated candle for Mike Salmon for years. Now her idol was not only dead, murdered, but his feet of clay were being ruthlessly exposed by these girls.

"None of this will be going to air, of course," declared Gloria. "We keep our dirty laundry in-house."

"If any of the ladies have a story to tell the police, they should be telling it," stated Gordon, firmly.

"Too right! I know I will," agreed Angelika.

Gloria pursed her lips. She too had held Mike in high regard, and was only now realizing that she might have been turning a blind eye to his failings. What else might she have missed?

"Yes, of course the police must hear of your experiences."

The station manager wasn't the only one in the room to be wondering if Salmon had perhaps overstepped the mark with the wrong person. Or a person with the wrong partner.

"But I don't think such things need be, or should be, broadcast," she said.

"A scandal would be bad for business," said Desley, making an effort to be professional.

That was inarguably true. After more discussion it was finally agreed that a brief statement was to be read out during the next morning's breakfast show. Yes, and during your program, too, Fitzroy. And during drive-time, currently being staffed on a rotating roster until Gloria could find a permanent new announcer.

"CRD-FM regrets to announce the passing of popular announcer Mike Salmon. Regular listeners will be aware that Mike has been away from the studio for some time. Everyone at the station was saddened to learn of his demise, which occurred during his absence. CRD-FM sends condolences to his family, and sympathies to his loyal listeners, many of whom will feel like they've lost a friend," read Gordon, practicing.

He kept a commendably straight face and even tone.

"Fine," said Gloria. "That can go to air tomorrow. The police interviews will be conducted in this room, commencing in – uh – a little over ten minutes. I shall be first. The rest of you, please consult the roster I gave out earlier, and stay nearby until you've been spoken to."

"Class dismissed," muttered Fitzroy petulantly.

As the staff filed out, they saw Detective Sergeant Sterling already in the reception area, already drumming his fingers impatiently on the 'Meeting In Progress' sign. He'd taken this round of interviews on while Mulholland was following up on the Dunbar and District Players. Bob had even less tolerance for, or patience with, thespian types than he did for or with "bloody old people." He was going to be absolutely delighted with Fitzroy Carlton.

INDEED, that was almost the first thing Sterling said later that afternoon when he met his detective at the police station.

"That old geezer on the radio is as mad as a cut snake! I mean, most of them are a bit odd, but his trolley has really jumped the tracks. And what an ego! He managed to turn every single question I asked around, to be about himself. 'What was Mike Salmon like?' 'Oh, not as popular as me.' 'Did he have any enemies you know of?' 'Those of us in the public eye always have enemies. I myself know that there are many people who resent me. Jealous of my success.' I swear he was peeved that Salmon was killed and not him, 'cos he's more important!"

"Nothing useful from him, then, eh? Did you do any better with anyone else?" asked Rita.

"A bit. I reckon a couple of them were jealous of the dead bloke. Not crazy like the old guy. He's too long in the tooth to be a suspect, anyway. But the guy who's got Salmon's job now, I reckon he could be a bit of a hard case. Tough, if you pushed him the wrong way. He's an old country boy, and you don't want to cross them. One or two of the others might talk tough, especially the women, but he's the one I could imagine actually <u>doing</u> something about it."

That was unusual. Bob didn't often imagine anything. Although, when he did, it was usually unpleasant.

"But no actual leads, then?" Rita asked.

"Nah, not really. A couple of the girls reckoned he could be a bit sleazy sometimes, but that's no reason for a violent murder."

Mulholland was quiet for a moment, then suggested, "It might be, depending on who he was being sleazy with, or at. If that person complained to someone else, who cared about them…"

"Hmm. I see what you're getting at. Possible. I reckon he was a harmless old goat, but yeah, somebody could take it the wrong way. Take him too seriously."

"How serious did these girls seem?"

"They weren't real happy, admittedly."

"Was one of them Angelika Judd, by any chance?"

"Name sounds familiar. Yeah, I reckon so."

Sterling rarely took anything more than brief, scribbled notes, relying instead on his memory, which was less prodigious than he made out.

"She was on my list of theatre company interviewees, but I couldn't see her because she was being interviewed by you."

"Oh well, that worked out, then."

Rita went quiet again, before saying, "I heard remarks from different people that tally with what you were told about Mike Salmon. How he was sometimes – unsavoury. From young people – both boys and girls, and from older ones, like teachers."

"Teachers?"

"Yes, there are a couple involved in the group. One of them, Alan Strong, actually took over the lead role from Salmon when he disappeared."

"Really? That's interesting," said Sterling thoughtfully.

"I can't see that as a motive, sir. The lead role in an amateur dramatic society? It hardly seems likely."

"No more so than that the victim was a bit of a sleazebag. Hey, there's a thought! A double motive. Get that juicy role, <u>and</u> thinking one of the kids actually had an issue with the old guy. If he's one of those caring, bleeding-heart types of teacher, and if he's an actor I reckon he probably is, that might fit together."

Rita silently opened her notebook. 'The man really does think in stereotypes. Individual personalities are lost on him. If he ever does jigsaws, I bet he uses a hammer instead of looking at the pieces...'

"Here we are. Alan Strong. Single. A career teacher, does seem to take a genuine interest in the students..."

"Yep, thought so. Just the type."

"He's not the only teacher, or ex-teacher in the group, though, sir. Poor Mr. Beaumaris, who just lost his wife and son, is also there."

"But this Strong bloke is the one who picked up the starring role."

"There is something else for us to consider, sir."

"What's that?"

"We have three dead bodies, all with the same unknown drug in their systems. In increasing quantities. What connects the three victims?"

"Mm, let me think... you may have already hit on it, Detective!"

"What?"

"That teacher, Beaumaris. His son's dead, and <u>he's</u> connected to the theatre mob."

Rita raised her eyebrows. "Yes, I suppose. But what about Solomona? Were the Beaumarises, father or son, connected with the football club?"

"Ah, no. I'm pretty sure they weren't. Damn. There's nothing to link all three of them."

"Beg your pardon, sir, but there is one obvious connection between them."

"Eh? What?"

"Trevor Salmon."

Sterling's frown deepened. There – it had been said. He probably <u>had</u> seen it, but didn't want to admit it, even to himself.

Reluctantly he said, "Yes. You're right. I can't imagine it, myself. Trevor's a good Club man, respected community figure. But you are right. He <u>will</u> have to be asked more questions. Get him in, and talk to him. You'll have to do it. I've known Trev too long, through the Club. It could be seen too much like a conflict of interest if I did the questioning."

"Alright, sir. I'll get onto him first thing tomorrow and try to get him in as soon as possible. At least I've spoken with him before. He shouldn't be too surprised to hear from me again."

"Good. When you've teed something up, let me know right away," said the Detective Sergeant. 'So that I can arrange to be somewhere else,' is what he didn't say.

.ooo.

26

The CEO's office at the Shelley Bay headquarters of SageCorp was empty again. The secretary had been firmly told that the CEO would be at home, possibly for several days. There was an emphatic instruction that absolutely no calls, from anyone, were to be forwarded to him. She herself could leave urgent messages on his voicemail service, which he would endeavour to check daily. He may or may not reply. The young woman had gulped and said, "Yes, Mr. Salmon." What else could she do?

SageCorp's CEO was, indeed, at home in his beach house, where he'd convened another meeting of the principals of his 'other' business – the one that was definitely more lucrative than his greyhounds, and potentially even more than land development, given time.

"Time, boys, is not our friend at the moment. It seems to have conspired against us. I've got the police leaving messages at my office, wanting to talk to me about the death of one of my employees. I presume it was that boy who wrapped his car around a tree so publicly."

"That wasn't my fault, boss! I wasn't to know he'd be stupid enough to drive with it in his system!"

"I understand that, Jonny, and I don't blame you. It was an unfortunate accident, that's all. Unfortunate for us, on top of Tuafeulaki's death, and the lamentable discovery of Mike's remains."

"How did that happen?" asked Graeme. "I was real careful this time. I tied a big weight to his leg before I dropped him over the side, so he wouldn't drift away like the first time, when we figured the rug he was rolled in would be heavy enough."

"By the looks of his body when I identified him, a shark bit off the leg that the weight was attached to. Again, unfortunate."

Darryl Frankem looked sour. "The way our luck's running, the same thing would have happened even if we <u>had</u> taken the time to do the job properly," he said.

Ronny looked as unhappy as his brother. He hadn't been blamed for anything yet, but it seemed inevitable. "I don't get how he washed ashore in the first place. We was miles out to sea when the party was on and your brother went – strange."

"Strange? Hah!" barked Graeme. "He tore all his clothes off and started running around the boat in the nudd, shouting and yelling!"

"I <u>did</u> say that Major Happy could affect different people in different ways, and the fool took more than he should have, anyway," said Frankem defensively.

"It scared the hell out of some of the guys in the team, and their girls," recalled Ronny.

"I remember having to calm a few down," admitted Darryl. "Reassure them that Mike was having a medical incident, and had gone below for a lie down. Any of them that wondered about him going 'off air' immediately afterwards should have chalked it up to the illness. Or to embarrassment."

Looking up from the dot point notes which he'd been making, Trevor nodded. "Which is why I got him down into the cabin as quickly as possible. That only made him worse. Started ranting and raving about never agreeing with getting into the drug business anyway. Madman actually attacked me!"

"You had to defend yourself, boss!" declared Ronny, loyally.

"With your grandfather's old gaff, that you kept on the boat," added Darryl, carefully neutral.

"It's my fault," admitted Salmon. "I'm too sentimental. I suppose I should have tossed it overboard, like Mike, but it's a family heirloom. It seemed appropriate to put it in the Museum one evening when nobody was around. Uncredited, alas, but whenever I saw it, I'd think of my grandfather."

"Not your brother," said Frankem flatly.

"No. As to your question, Ron, I can only assume that the corpse was somehow dislodged from the carpet, caught, and carried by a strong current generated by the storms we had. It was only lucky that we came across the remains of the rug and knew to go looking for him."

"That's about the only good luck we've had lately," said Darryl gloomily.

"That, and your rediscovering the body," agreed Trevor. "Although, now I think of it, even that has been a double-edged sword. I suppose it's not statistically unusual that someone else should find Michael before you did, but for that person to then be right alongside you, pursuing the same hobby... It _is_ lucky that he hasn't yet recognized you."

"_Yet_ is right," said Frankem. "I've avoided him as much as I can, without making it too obvious. I wish his wife hadn't been asking so many damned questions. He might have forgotten the whole thing, otherwise."

Graeme's expression darkened. He wasn't the brains of the outfit, but he knew that a witness wasn't a good thing. Especially one that might identify _him_.

The CEO didn't notice the expression, and was consulting his notes. "First and foremost, we need to be away from here for a little while, until the police interest blows over."

"You reckon it will, boss?" asked Jonny, uncertainly.

"I'm sure of it. I know Bob Sterling, and I doubt that he can _spell_ 'persistence'. He may want to talk to me now, but if he can't , within a few days he'll have found an easier suspect. One more readily connected with that dead boy. He'll fixate on them, and find a way to make a charge stick. We'll discreetly return in a few weeks or so, be delighted to hear that the matter is resolved, and get on with our lives and business."

The others nodded, some slowly. None of them liked to argue with Salmon at the best of times, and he did sound confident.

"There's nothing to link us with the drug in any way, is there, Darryl?"

"I don't believe so. It was conceived as a drug for greyhounds, to influence race results. The thought that it may have other applications was an unexpected realization."

"I remember those early conversations," said Trevor, almost wistfully. "Inspirational."

"It didn't hurt to have a ready supply of test subjects," added the vet casually.

Both Lofton brothers looked unhappy at this description of their workmates and teammates respectively.

"But no," continued Frankem, regardless. "There should be nothing in that young driver's body that can be linked to us in any way. The drug could have been obtained from anywhere."

"What about in my brother?"

"With the amount of time his body spent in the ocean, we'd have to be very unlucky indeed for there to be anything left for anyone to find," replied Darryl.

"Good enough for me," said Trevor.

"What about Solly?" asked Ronny. "He might have had some Major Happy in his system."

"Really?" asked Trevor. He pondered for a moment or two. "He wasn't on a strong dose. When was he last provided with some?"

"On that boat trip, at the party," said Ronny. "He seemed a bit withdrawn. Not really the partying type, so I slipped him a little to loosen him up. I don't reckon he had any at home – that's how I got him up to the lookout later. To give him a new supply, 'cos he told me at training he'd run out."

Salmon sighed. "It's a real pity he wasn't more involved in the festivities. He might not have been awake enough to notice a rolled-up rug being thrown overboard, then ask questions when we got back to shore. I'd thought he had potential. Darryl, how long would the drug remain in his system?"

The vet shrugged. "The effect itself doesn't last long. There'd probably be minute traces for a few days, depending on the size of that last dose. It was designed for animals, remember. The only post mortem testing I got to do was on dogs, not humans, unfortunately."

The Lofton brothers exchanged unhappy looks again.

Trevor pursed his lips. "Another bit of bad luck. Another reason to keep our profile low. Fortunately, Solomona wasn't involved in the construction part of the business, so there's nothing to connect him to the other boy."

"He knew me. Worked with the dogs, sometimes," Frankem pointed out.

"True, but the one in the car had no link to you. And otherwise, the Tongan was just a footballer."

Ronny winced a little at that, as Trevor blithely moved on to another dot point.

"That brings me neatly to my next item. Jonah Latukefu. As contrite as he seemed when I last spoke with him, after that unfortunate incident at the Burrawidgee game, I still fear he's a loose cannon. I doubt he has the stability to stand up to any intense questioning if the police decide to re-interview any of the Demons."

"Is that likely, do you reckon?" asked Ronny nervously.

"It's possible, in my absence. Sterling will be looking for someone to blame. I think Jonah should join us on our little cruise. I'm sure he'll enjoy the Great Barrier Reef."

"That's where we're going? Great!" said Graeme.

"For a start, at least. Possibly further, if the mood takes us. The boat is well equipped. Speaking of which – next point: Darryl, I want you to move your laboratory equipment on board."

"All of it?"

"Whatever is necessary for manufacture. Anything else which may have been... tainted, by previous work, is to be disposed of. Thoroughly, and in a location completely unrelated and unrelatable to any of us. Clear?"

"Totally. When do we leave?"

"As soon as possible. As soon as Ron and Jon can bring our other guest here – quietly, boys. Even his brother is not to know. And as soon as you can take care of your equipment and supplies, Darryl. Graeme can help you. Ideally, this afternoon or evening. I'll let my housekeeper know I'll be away for a while. She's used to that. She comes in once per week to stop the dust accumulating, and the gardener drops by fortnightly, so the place won't look obviously deserted."

Salmon looked about the room. "Right, men, you have your tasks. Pack for yourselves, then be about them."

Clearly, they were dismissed, and no more questions were encouraged. The four men departed quickly, allowing Trevor to go about his own packing and preparations. He was as calm as any businessman about to go on a leisurely vacation. He had everything organized, and was supremely confident in his own abilities.

.ooo.

27

She really hoped that her sigh wasn't audible down the phone. Shauna Shallacot had been expecting this call. Dreading it, but expecting it. Was there a curse on *Sweeney Todd - the Musical*, or was it just on her?

"Of course, Tom, I entirely understand. Of course, I'd love you to stay with your theatre family and let us do all we can to support – oh, sorry, yes. A poor choice of words, I do apologize."

Beaumaris spoke quietly again.

"No, I do see," she replied. "You couldn't be expected to concentrate on your performance with so much else on your mind. No, Tom. If you're sure... yes. We can manage. I appreciate your being professional enough to call me and explain. Yes, Tom. You should go and do whatever it is that you feel you have to, absolutely. Good luck with it. Goodbye, Tom."

'Damn and blast,' the director thought. Time to review the cast list, <u>again</u>.

Tom Beaumaris gazed thoughtfully at his phone. Even amateur actors should behave professionally, he believed, and it was gratifying that Shauna recognized that he'd done so. A part of him really did hate to leave the production, especially so late in rehearsals. He'd been enjoying the role, and the company. It was mostly easy-going, friendly and supportive. One or two people he <u>really</u> liked, and could talk to...

On impulse, he consulted his contact list, and called one particular crew member.

"Hello, Cianawyn Lauder, can I help you? Oh! Tom! How are you feeling? Arthur and I have been thinking of you. I did leave a message, but when you didn't reply I didn't want to risk disturbing you..."

"It's okay Shan-win. I did appreciate your calling. Sorry, I should have called you back, but I've just had so much on my mind."

"I'm sure you have. Is there anything that we can do for you? Any help with anything?"

"That's a kind offer, but no, thanks. I've got myself pretty well sorted out."

"Good."

"I've quit *Sweeney Todd*, I'm afraid."

"That <u>is</u> a shame. I think you've been very good, and a pleasure to work with. But if I'm honest, I'm not surprised at your decision. How did Shauna take it?"

"Pretty well. I think she was at least half-expecting it, too. She did suggest the show might be a good distraction for me."

"That could be true, you know."

"It could, yes. But I don't want to be distracted. I've got things to do. A thing. And it's important."

"As long as you're sure, Tom."

"Very. I guess that's why I called you, though. I wanted to talk to someone, and you listen better than anyone I know. Better even than Laura used to."

"Oh, Tom..."

"No, I mean it. I loved Laura every day of our lives together. I still do. But sometimes she'd drift off in the middle of a conversation. 'Bright shiny object' syndrome, she used to call it."

Cianawyn couldn't help but laugh. "I'm afraid most people do that from time to time. I know Arthur and I both do," she admitted.

"Never in my experience. Not you," said Tom. "Whenever we've talked, I've always felt like I had your full attention, and I deeply appreciate that."

"You're very welcome, Tom. You're a good man, and very easy to talk with."

"Thank you, Shan-win," he said, before hanging up suddenly.

"That was not good," she told Arthur, who'd been engrossed in a crossword as he assiduously avoided listening in to what he'd taken to be a private conversation.

"What isn't?" he asked.

She explained the gist of the call.

"That's a damn shame," said her husband sympathetically. "I like Tom. He's a nice bloke."

"Very. He didn't deserve something like this to happen."

"I don't reckon many people do, sweetheart." He looked at his darling bride's glum face. "I reckon we both need something to cheer us up. How about I take us out for an ice cream?"

"It's not the weather for it, hon. Have you looked outside? The rain's started again."

But Arthur was not to be deterred, and he knew the way to his wife's heart. "Moroccan mint tea and baklava," he declared. "The Marrakesh doesn't shut until four."

For a moment, Cianawyn was about to argue, but she paused. She saw the look on his face, and she allowed herself to stop and think. A distraction would be good, yes. And the Marrakesh was a rare treat.

"Okay, why not? We can get a table inside," she replied gratefully. "Exactly what we need. Good idea, babe, it'll be good for us both."

.ooo.

28

─────

The Marrakesh was on the fringe of Dunbar's CBD. It was a small enterprise, part café and part restaurant, according to the time of day or evening. At the moment, it was in café mode, specializing in pastries, coffee (their Turkish was excellent), and a range of teas.

The Moroccan mint was a house specialty, and Cianawyn Lauder was a big fan of it. She dabbed flaky pastry crumbs from the corner of her mouth and smiled at her husband.

"This was a good idea, hon," she said. "Thanks."

"You're welcome, my love," he replied.

They finished their teas in companionable silence. Ordinarily they'd prefer to dine there alfresco, but there had been intermittent heavy rain all day.

"It's a shame," Cianawyn said, "I'd have quite liked a wander through town. Do some window shopping."

"We've already got all the windows we need," replied Arthur. "I'm sure you'd rather look at shoes and bags."

She scrunched up her napkin and threw it at him.

"Seriously," he continued. "The rain's eased off for the moment. It would be good for both of us to walk off the baklava."

She shrugged. He <u>was</u> right. "Okay, let's do it," she said.

Bayer had already paid for everything when he'd ordered, so they were able to stroll straight out onto the main street. At a leisurely pace, they ambled towards the centre of town. Dunbar was usually quiet at this hour of the afternoon anyway, but the weather made it even more so.

The rain was now a light drizzle, but neither were bothered. Cianawyn wore a light waterproof jacket, and her husband rarely cared about getting at least a bit wet. They looked in shop windows, patted friendly dogs, and did some casual people watching as they made their way along the street.

"Oh! I'd like to just duck in here for a minute or two," said Cianawyn, indicating a small boutique that she was fond of.

"No worries. I'll wait out here," her beau replied.

It was a frequent port of call. Arthur knew the shop was cramped, and that there was nowhere for an uninvolved spouse to sit. Hanging around outside the changing rooms only attracted suspicious looks from customers and staff, he'd found.

"Thanks, hon."

There was a tree to keep the worst of the rain off as he stood, humming to himself and people watching. A busker, brave and presumably weatherproof, playing an out-of-tune guitar under a shop awning across the road and up the street. A surprisingly steady, if intermittent stream of cars. A grumbling mother shepherding her three equally grumpy children past a posh toy store. A mismatched pair of men, one little, one large, apparently having a trivial argument as they walked along.

Wait on - those two were familiar... Yes! The oversized rain hat on the smaller man was the clincher. He'd met these two on Cemetery Beach. Brow furrowed, he stepped forward to intercept them. Before he could speak, the smaller man looked up to see who was in his way.

"Oh. Hello, Arthur," he said.

"Darryl! I didn't recognize you!"

"Hah ha – no, I imagine not. Take any of us out of the context of the theatre, and we all go back to being ordinary folks, don't we?"

"Yeah. Yeah, I guess that's true, isn't it?" Arthur paused. "But now... Darryl... now I know where I've seen you before. Before *Sweeney Todd*, even."

What happened next happened very fast. For Arthur, especially, it was a blur.

Big Graeme had run at him from behind, palms extended, and slammed his substantial weight into the small of Arthur's back. The impact sent the older man flying off the footpath and onto the street, right into the path of a large, oncoming SUV. Luckily, the driver had been doing a very sedate pace, and even on the wet road was able to stop before running over the prone figure. The reason he'd been driving slowly was that he'd glanced in his rear-view mirror and realized that there was a police car travelling right behind him – always a good incentive for motoring caution.

One occupant of the police car was Sergeant Chris Derbishire. He told the constable who was driving to pull over as soon as practical, but while the car was stationary behind the SUV, he jumped out and started to run. He'd seen what had happened, heard and seen Cianawyn shout and run out of the shop, from where she'd been a witness to the last few moments. Satisfied that she would take care of her husband, at least for the moment, he took off after the lumbering Graeme Mount.

Meanwhile, Darryl Frankem ran in the opposite direction, much more speedily than his erstwhile companion. He was cursing furiously, knowing that Trevor would be likewise irate. This was why they'd never given Major Happy to Graeme, he thought. The fat thug was already impulsive. The drug would have made him even more unstable and unpredictable. Damn, damn, damn...

The police sergeant wasn't much more than half the weight of the man he was pursuing, but he was much tougher than often given credit for. Getting his timing just right, he launched himself into a flying tackle around the chubby legs. During the years that Graeme had played rugby league, he'd often had smaller men tackle him, or attempt to. Few had ever done so as effectively as Derbishire now did.

Mount tried to use his footballing experience to land well, but his reflexes were slower than they used to be, and the paved footpath was less forgiving than a muddy football field. All he achieved was to bruise one forearm, and crack the other elbow hard onto the concrete. There would turn out to be a fracture there when anyone eventually bothered to look.

Back along the street, Cianawyn knelt by the prostrate figure of her beloved. He was conscious, but groaning, and not lucid enough to make clear where the pain was. The SUV had managed to get around him and into a convenient parking bay. Its driver was now hovering nearby, a worried expression on his face.

The police car had been rolled further forward, providing some protection for Arthur. The young constable had called for an ambulance before checking briefly on the injured man, then directing traffic around him and the police car.

Sergeant Derbishire returned, propelling the would-be fugitive just in front of him. Given their relative sizes, it might have looked incongruously funny, were it not for the expressions on the two men's faces.

Mount, his hands cuffed behind him, was trying to appear characteristically surly, but couldn't escape looking like he feared the sky falling down on him at any moment. It wasn't fear of the police etched on his face, but the dark anticipation of Trevor Salmon's reaction.

For his part, Chris was glaring daggers at the big man's back. He liked Arthur Bayer, and was going to ensure that there'd be trouble over this assault. Probably an attempted murder charge, if he could convince Sterling to go to that much effort, and he would certainly try.

He called to the other policeman, "Hayden! Lock this slug in the back of the car securely, and call for backup to haul him in ASAP. Have you called the medics?"

"Yes, sarge. They're on their way."

"Good man. Then keep watching the traffic, keep them moving. I'll see how Mr. Bayer and his wife are doing."

Graeme was propelled into the back seat of the police car with no courtesy, but all possible care to see that he couldn't go anywhere.

Chris squatted on the street beside the victim. "How are you, Arthur?"

"Sore," was the answer through clenched teeth.

"Ms Lauder?" the sergeant asked, turning to the worried wife.

"It's his back," she said. "I <u>think</u> he can move his legs, but there doesn't seem to be much feeling in his arms, the right one especially."

"Bugger," said the policeman softly. "The ambulance is on its way, folks. Try to hang on. I want to get some details from this witness – let him be on his way – and I'll be right back."

Derbishire was as good as his word. He took the witness' name and phone number, and a brief account of what he'd seen. It tallied with his own view of events.

Constable Hayden was doing his best to manage the traffic flow (not that there was a lot in Dunbar on a wet afternoon) while keeping an eye on the miscreant in the back of the car. The big man didn't look like much of a threat now. He was slumped forward, his broad bovine forehead propped against the back of the driver's seat.

Hayden couldn't see his face, but would have been reassured if he had. No trace of anger remained. Graeme just looked disconsolate. It wasn't that he regretted his impulsive action. All he regretted was getting caught.

Derbishire again squatted beside Cianawyn, doing his best to reassure her as she stroked Arthur's arm, fretting that he couldn't feel her touch.

"Hang in there, Ms Lauder. I reckon your fella's a fighter," the policeman said.

"Rather be a lover," Bayer managed to rasp out.

"Ay! You must be feeling better – you're making bad jokes!"

"Know I'm in real... trouble, if I... ever stop... doing that," he managed. What he <u>was</u> doing was trying to reassure his darling bride.

Chris noticed, though, that he still wasn't moving. 'Doesn't want to, or can't?' he worried.

The second police car and the ambulance arrived almost simultaneously. Mount was moved to the other car, none too gently, and was whisked away to be put in a cell, awaiting at least an attempted manslaughter charge, and more if Derbishire could make it happen.

The ambulance crew, after a careful examination, moved Arthur gently onto a backboard and into their vehicle. As they worked, Arthur distracted himself by explaining to the police sergeant the little that he knew.

He'd seen Darryl Frankem and his corpulent companion, and suddenly recognized them from the incident at Cemetery Beach. He'd been speaking with Frankem, then suddenly went flying.

"By chance, I saw that," said Chris. "I saw the big bloke deliberately run into your back and shove you out onto the road."

One of the medics said to Arthur, "You're lucky, I think. We won't know until the scans, but I don't there's severe spinal cord damage. Not even broken bones, fingers crossed. There's going to be one hell of a bruise, and I think there's a nasty whiplash injury, but it could have been a whole lot worse."

"I think it was meant to be," murmured Arthur as the mild painkilling injection kicked in. He slipped into a blessedly dreamless sleep.

.ooo.

29

––––––––––

The term 'Happy Hour' had seemed inappropriate to Callie this particular Friday evening, with the news that her favourite son-in-law (the only one, mind you) was in hospital, possibly suffering from spinal injuries.

After a call from his son, Kenneth Derbishire had taken it upon himself to get her to the Watering Hole, keeping them both dry by going the short distance in the car he now rarely used. It was obvious that she was upset, and he rightly figured that the distraction of conversation would be better for her than sitting fretting in her room.

So, the two of them joined Dolly, Dawn and Jim at their regular table. Without going into too much of the detail that she'd gotten from her daughter, Callie explained what was happening with 'the youngsters'. There were a lot of sympathetic "oh, no" and "tsk-tsk" exclamations from the others.

"And I'd been in such a cheerful mood, too, despite the weather," said Callie concluded.

"How about you tell us what you were so cheery about?" suggested Kenneth, shrewdly.

"Yes, good idea," she replied, patting his hand without noticing. "This will be meaningful to you, Dolly. For you others, please bear with me, and I'll explain in a minute. I got a call earlier today from Georgie Fletcher. She's spoken to her parents at last. Reassured them that she's well, happy, and busy. She rang me to say that she's got a surprise for them. Asked me if I thought it would be 'okay' if she sent them two tickets for Opening Night of the show she's doing at the Arcadium. She was worried about them affording the trip to Sydney."

"Ooh, that's lovely!" enthused Dolly. "The Arcadium! I always knew that young 'un had some talent. Ooh, I'm so bleedin' <u>proud</u> of her!"

The smile was back on Callie's face as she said, "Yes, I am too. Silly – I've never even actually <u>met</u> the young lady."

"There's never anything silly about caring for other people," Jim reminded her.

"Quite right," agreed Kenneth. "You're to be commended for the effort I think you did, on her behalf."

"Her parents, really," Callie admitted.

"And that's a lovely thing," said Dolly. "I know how upset they both was."

"I was going to ask Cianawyn and Arthur to drive me over tomorrow, to tell them face-to-face. But now, well, I suppose I'll just have to call them. I've still not actually met either of the Fletchers, as far as I know."

"Young Shan should be available in a day or two, pet, I'm sure. But if you don't want to wait, I could drive you there and introduce you. I've known Mary and Neil since Georgie was a little tyke."

"That's a nice offer," said Jim. "I'm sure it would do some good for everyone involved."

Jim Cooke may not have known the details, but he was a generous-hearted man, and he read the feeling around the table.

"Be glad to help. I really do 'ope young Arthur is okay. I know I'm being selfish, but the play can't afford to lose anyone else," said the musical director, apologetically.

"I think our Mr. Bayer is a good deal tougher than he's given credit for," said Jim, encouragingly. "There's resilience under that affable exterior.

That won a proud smile from Cailleach Steele. "I do believe you're right, Jim," she said.

Dawn patted Jim's arm supportively. Since his debut as a volunteer at the Fishing Museum, the quiet affection between the two of them had slowly become a little more public.

Perhaps recalling that day, Kenneth brought up another subject. "I don't know if you've heard – I don't know if it's public yet, but I know the four of you are discreet. That body that Arthur found washed up, that was Mike Salmon."

"Ah – I did wonder when I heard that snippet on the radio," said Dawn.

"But there's more." Kenneth's voice was quiet, so as not to carry beyond their table. "Chris tells me that Salmon was murdered, and very probably by that weapon that was brought in from the Museum."

"How awful!" exclaimed Callie, with Dolly and Dawn making similar sounds of shock and agreement.

It was Jim who didn't look surprised, only thoughtful. "That makes sense," he finally said. "I asked around the other volunteers, and it turns out that nobody actually knew where it had come from. It hadn't been part of the display a few months earlier, when the last property audit was done. It seems to have just... appeared, one day, without anyone noticing."

"Hiding in plain sight," said Kenneth.

"An old trick, but still an effective one," observed Callie.

"Who could have done it?" asked Dawn.

Jim spread his hands. "Anyone who has a key. The most senior volunteers. Shift supervisors. Cleaners. Even the Board members."

"I expect all of them will be being asked some questions by the police," said Kenneth, evenly.

"I certainly hope so," agreed Callie.

NIGHT TIMES WERE quiet at the school. The kids were long gone, office staff and teachers leaving at later intervals, according to their workloads. Even the cleaners came and went before the darkness got too deep. And it <u>was</u> deep tonight, heavy cloud obscuring the starlight.

Those cleaners had keys to every building. Only the headmistress, her deputy, and the head of Administration shared that level of access. The most senior teachers had access to their own classrooms and facilities.

For Tom Beaumaris, that included his chemistry lab. He worked silently, his concentration focussed like a laser. He was mixing a cocktail that any of his students potentially could have, if they'd been taught certain things. Mind you, any teacher caught providing such instruction ought to be promptly dismissed. Tom knew that, and greatly respected it. A little knowledge was a dangerous thing. Sometimes, though, a lot of knowledge could be even more dangerous.

There was no turmoil or agitation in Tom's brain. In many ways, he was thinking more clearly and calmly than he'd ever done in his life.

The Detective Sergeant had called to tell him about the drug found in his son's body, and had asked bluntly if Tom knew its origins. He didn't, and at that moment, hadn't hazarded a guess. Soon afterward, though, as he sat in the now painfully lonely front room of his house, pieces fell together.

Off-hand remarks that Ted had made, about how Jonny Lofton had helped him 'in lots of ways.' How Jonny had 'given him so much'. How he'd worried at first, but it was really working out. And how 'it' really came from the big boss, Mr. Salmon, so it must be okay.

The autopsy finding had suddenly made clear what 'it' was, in a general sense at least.

Tom had met Jonny Lofton a couple of times. He wasn't a stupid man, the teacher thought, but neither did he have the cleverness to run any sort of business. Not building, and not drugs. That required a certain sort of brains. The sort that could build up a development company like SageCorp. The sort that Trevor Salmon possessed.

No part of the old building which housed the Dunbar Police Station was especially salubrious. The basement holding cells were among the least inviting areas, second only to the men's toilets reserved for members of the public (the Ladies' were much newer).

One such cell was occupied by Graeme Mount, whose personal space was currently being invaded by the angry Detective Sergeant. It wasn't that Bob had any affection for Arthur Bayer, far from it. But recent events had worn through the meagre tissue of his patience. And now, here was a crook whose identity and actions required no investigation, as far as he was concerned. All he wanted was an answer to the question, "Why?".

He knew Mount from the football club. Not well, admittedly, but well enough to know he was a meathead, a thug, and a bully. If there's one thing a bully dislikes, it's another, bigger, bully. Mount wasn't saying much, though.

That was all due to Trevor Salmon. Graeme was torn. He trusted that Trevor, whose bidding he'd faithfully done for a long time, would somehow get him out of this, so he didn't want to admit to anything that might make matters worse.

On the other hand, he was genuinely fearful of Salmon's reaction if he felt in any way betrayed. He'd seen the boss angry before, and this blonde pretty-boy copper had nothing on him. For one thing, Graeme knew that the police weren't allowed to use the same tactics as the CEO. Well, legally, neither was Trevor of course, but if nobody knew, then nobody cared, and nobody stopped him.

Either way, Graeme was stubbornly silent. He hadn't even so much as mentioned Trevor's name, just in case. That stubbornness, and the claustrophobic little cell, had worn through Sterling's meagre reserve of patience, but even he knew that there were limits on what he could do to obtain information – just as Graeme understood.

Frustrated, Sterling stormed out of the cell, slamming the door shut behind him. Mount didn't react at all.

Back upstairs, the Detective Sergeant sat at his desk and seethed.

Rita Mulholland brought him a terrible coffee (not her fault, the station only had a cheap instant powder) and let him vent his aggravation.

After some time of this, she suggested, "Let's try bringing him up here and questioning him."

"You reckon you can do better, do you?" snapped Sterling angrily.

"It's not that. You don't like working in the cell. It doesn't seem to affect him. I'm just suggesting that a different environment may get different results. You'd be more comfortable, and maybe he'd be less so, where more people can see him."

"Mm. Makes sense," Bob admitted.

A very short time later, Graeme Mount was sitting in a corner of Sterling's office, hands again cuffed behind his back. He was known officially to have committed a violent crime, and unofficially to have a violent, impulsive temper, so no chances were being taken.

The Detective Sergeant sat behind the desk that Mulholland stood leaning her hip against, idly reading the case file.

"Enjoy the view from that window, Mr. Mount," she said, knowing he was at the wrong height and angle to see more than a section of blank wall. "It's the best view you'll have for a long time."

"Not saying nothing," was the reply.

"Suit yourself. There is zero prospect of you being found not guilty. Too many witnesses. The only thing at question is the length of your sentence. That will depend on whether you go down for attempted manslaughter, or more likely, attempted murder. Tell us why you attacked Mr. Bayer, and you might just get the lower charge."

"Not saying nothing."

"Mount, you're a mug," said Sterling. "You're still entitled to a phone call. Do you want to keep trying that same number that isn't answering? Or now, maybe, a lawyer?"

The number was, of course, Trevor's. In Graeme's mind, Salmon was still his best, maybe only, hope. They had nothing on the boss, knew nothing about anything. He would have smirked, if he wasn't in such an awkward spot himself.

"Would you like a coffee, boss?" asked Rita casually.

"Eh? Wha- oh, sure."

A few minutes later, both detectives were sitting quietly, sipping their coffee, doing their best to look like they were enjoying it. Importantly, the aroma of the coffee was wafting over Graeme Mount. What he'd been served in the cell during his stay had mostly been water or weak orange cordial. As Mulholland had surmised, the scent of the coffee was having more of an effect on the prisoner than the questions of either officer.

Suddenly, there was a knock on the office door. At a word from Sterling, the door opened and the coroner, Dr. Cartwright, walked in. There was a look of deep concern on her face.

"You wanted me to tell you when I had more information about the drug found in the three bodies. Well, I've been doing a lot of work on it, and I think I can give you some answers," she announced.

Sterling was about to say something like, "About time," but Mulholland got in first.

"Well done, Doc. I'm sure it will prove worth the wait! What have you got?" As she spoke, Rita stood and ushered the doctor into her chair. The detective resumed her spot standing by the desk, while Cartwright consulted her notes.

"I'm still not sure of absolutely everything that's in this drug, but there are a few things that I <u>can</u> tell you. As I indicated earlier, at its base is ketamine. As you know, that's used as a 'date rape' drug."

"It reduces the victim's resistance, right?" asked Rita.

"In a way, yes. It makes a person less inhibited. On its own, it can act as a sedative, or it can have the opposite effect on some people for a spell before the relaxant kicks in. As I've said, what we have here is a cocktail. A dangerous one, I believe." The coroner wasn't cold, but she was dispassionate.

"Three deaths would suggest that," said Sterling drily.

"Indeed, but not what I'm getting at. The drug may have been involved in any or all of those deaths. I don't know, I'm not a detective. But it wasn't the direct cause of death. However, among its ingredients are some surprising things like nicotine and even caffeine."

"Eh?" the D.S. looked baffled.

"Many drugs are what we call behaviourally addictive," Cartwright explained. "The user craves the effect. The high, or the low, whatever, and so builds up a pattern of use or abuse to get that effect as often as possible. It becomes a psychological need. There are some drugs, though, that actually cause a physical dependency. They affect the body's chemistry in such a way that the person comes to rely on a particular chemical stimulus to function normally. Often, it's the brain that's affected, which can make it hard to distinguish the difference, but it's an important one."

Rita nodded thoughtfully. "I can see what you mean about dangerous."

"Such drugs are fundamentally toxic. More so than others – all of them are to some extent. But these are cumulative. An overdose could kill, as is true of almost anything if the dose is large enough. But these will kill slowly but surely as the poison builds up in the system."

"How long?" asked Sterling.

"It depends on the individual."

"It is a drug of dependency, then," said Rita.

"Very deliberately made that way, I'd say. Yes," the coroner confirmed.

"Any idea what the more, let's say, attractive effects might be?" Mulholland quizzed.

Graham Mount had been sitting staring at the wall while Cartwright spoke. Technicalities mostly went over his head.

The doctor started counting off possible responses on her fingers. "A general feeling of elation, though too mild to become hysteria. Reduced inhibition. Willingness to take risks that would normally be avoided. Possibly a greater tolerance of pain. Carelessness. It may make someone more prone to violence if they already have an aggressive nature."

"Yep, that sounds like Major Happy," the big man said, to everyone's surprise. He'd been so quiet as the coroner spoke that even Rita had momentarily forgotten he was in the room.

With an effort, Sterling kept his voice low and even as he asked, "Who, or what, is Major Happy?"

Suddenly Graeme realized that he'd just gotten himself into a whole new world of trouble.

The severity of the trouble was immediately revealed to him when Detective Mulholland added, "Besides being the drug found in three bodies recently."

If they knew about Major Happy, they must know everything, he reasoned (incorrectly – 'reason' wasn't Graeme's strength), in which case Trevor wouldn't be in any position to help him. His only chance was to help himself.

The big man sang like a canary. Mulholland's note-taking hand could barely keep up with him. Sterling said nothing, simply because he didn't need to.

.ooo.

30

A day after his 'encounter' with Frankem and Mount, Arthur was probably feeling better than his wife. His neck was in a soft brace, and his arm in a sling, but he'd been cleared of any major spinal damage, and with the aid of sedatives, he'd slept deeply.

Cianawyn, in a large chair beside his hospital bed, had also slept, but much less, and much less deeply. When she did close her eyes and drift off, she found herself reliving the drive behind the ambulance. Every nerve-wracking red light, twist and turn, imagining every sort of catastrophic diagnosis.

They'd been married for several years, but not their whole adult lives, and their time together had been free of major illness, accident or trauma. This was the closest either had come to losing the other, and it had been an enormous shock to her.

Right now he was attempting a crossword, with less success than usual (blame the drugs, he thought), while his beloved dozed fitfully in the big chair. Their peace and quiet was interrupted when Cianawyn's mobile phone suddenly rang.

She jumped and snatched at the phone, fearing that it had woken

Arthur as it had her. She looked at the incoming number and frowned.

"It's Tom Beaumaris," she said, surprised and worried. "Hello, Tom."

"Er - hello Shan-win. Sorry to bother you again."

"No bother, Tom. What can I do for you?"

"Um... listen, if you would, please. You're the only one left who does."

"Oh, Tom. Really, I..."

Beaumaris cut off her protest. "You should know. I'm going to kill Trevor Salmon."

Looking up from a puzzle book that he'd been distracting himself with, Arthur wondered why his darling bride had gone pale, her jaw hanging loosely.

"Ah, I beg your pardon, Tom..."

"I'm going to kill Trevor Salmon. I've realized he's responsible for killing my wife and only child. He's behind the drugs that were in Ted's system the day they died."

"Are you sure?" she asked, not doubting him, but seeking evidence.

"Certain. Added it all up from things that Ted had mentioned. Oh, I don't imagine Salmon sold him the stuff directly, but he was definitely the one in control of it."

Cianawyn's mind was racing. It did seem all too plausible, given what she'd heard of Trevor Salmon. And his brother, for that matter. Perhaps they'd been in it together.

"Tom – you didn't have anything to do with Mike's...?"

"Mike Salmon? No, I promise. I've no idea if he was involved in this or not. But I am one hundred percent sure about Trevor, and I'm going to get my revenge."

"What good will that do? It won't bring them back. Tom, you're my friend..."

"I know, Shan-win. That's why I'm telling you. Somebody needs to know, for afterwards. In case I'm not around to explain, and I might not be. I need to know that it's worked. Laura and Ted are gone,

Shan-win. They were my whole reason for living. Now, my only reason is to make absolutely sure that Trevor Salmon can't do the same to anyone else's family."

"You said yourself, he probably wasn't the one who sold Ted the drugs…"

By now, Arthur's full attention was on the one side of the conversation that he could hear.

"I know," said Tom. "But if you cut the head off a snake, it'll soon die."

"I'm afraid drug rings might be more like those mythological monsters, that can grow a new head if one's chopped off."

"Maybe, but that'll take time. And maybe Trevor's death will prompt the police to do some <u>proper</u> investigation into the whole thing. Bust it open completely. That's part of why I'm telling you. Did you know, one of those detectives was trying to make out that I knew about the supply of drugs in Dunbar? Me. Because I work at the school, and I'm involved in the theatre."

"I can guess who that was. When are you thinking of…?"

"Soon. After work tonight, I hope."

"You're at work?"

"Not my work, his. SageCorp's office will have security."

"If he's the criminal you think he is, and I don't disagree with you, I'm sure he has his own security everywhere."

"Probably. Which is part of why I don't really expect to come out of this alive myself. But I truly don't care about that."

"Look, Tom, I…"

"Sorry Shan-win. I know you want to, but I can't be talked out of this. Please, just remember what I've told you about my reason. Thanks for listening, now and before. God bless. Goodbye."

"Tom? Tom?"

He'd gone. She sat, staring at the phone.

"Sweetheart?" said Arthur, gently.

Her eyes glistening, Cianawyn related the call, in comprehensive detail. Finally, she asked, "Oh Ay – what should we do?"

"Do?" replied her beloved, vexingly blank.

"We have to stop him! How can we, though?"

"Hang on a moment, darling. Why do we 'have to' stop him? You've said yourself that Salmon is probably as guilty as Tom thinks. Of this, and who knows what else, based on what we've heard and talked about."

"That's not the point. That's why we have laws, and a justice system."

"And don't they work brilliantly? Especially on people who have plenty of money. Darling, there are convicted criminals running whole countries."

"But people can't just take matters into their own hands."

"Not even victims? Who can't see any prospect of justice being done?"

There was silence for some time, as both thought deeply. Arthur's words had at least paused his wife from hasty action.

Suddenly Arthur pressed his Nurse Call button.

"Ay! What's wrong?"

"Nothing, darling. Hand me my clothes, please. Once a nurse takes this needle out of my arm, we can get out of here."

"What…"

"I'm discharging myself. The doctor's already said that I can go home when I feel up to it, if I'm careful. Well, I do, and I will be."

"But, hon…"

"No buts, sweetheart. I understand how upset you are about Tom, so let's do something about it."

"What do you suggest?"

"We try to stop him. Talk him out of it. That's what you want, right?"

"Well, yes – but my main concern is you," said Cianawyn, the worry very evident in her voice.

"As long as you don't mind driving, I'll be fine. I might not be up for a fight, or even a chase, but I can talk. Stick a foot out and trip someone trying to run past. Throw stuff, if it'll help. But mostly, talk."

Cianawyn bent and kissed her husband. "Thank you for reminding me why I love you," she said softly.

"You're welcome, sweetheart. Ah! Nurse Moss – thanks..."

Removing Arthur's cannula was the easy bit – the nurse was brisk and efficient. Hospital administration, alas, was rather less so, and it took almost another hour before enough paperwork had been completed to allow the patient to take his leave.

At least that gave the couple time to make some sort of plan.

"Tom said he'd go for the kill after SageCorp closes for the day, so he must know where Trevor lives," said Arthur.

"We know it's an old place in the Dunes. Someone in *Sweeney Todd* mentioned that. But the Dunes is a pretty big area."

"Yeah. We can't really just drive around and hope that we spot Tom's car. What we need is Salmon's address. It's a pity we don't have a phone book, but I don't think they even get printed these days."

"Maybe not," said Cianawyn, "I do know where to find one, though."

At the end of the corridor was the Visitors' Lounge for that ward. It wasn't very inviting. Cramped and cluttered. The television produced no sound, and its pictures were too fuzzy to be watchable. The newest of the magazines had a cover date from the previous decade, and the oldest was a *National Geographic* from 1983. The Dunbar District phone book which gathered dust on a bookshelf alongside two Gideons Bibles was only five years old.

The address of the old Salmon family holiday home was in there, along with a phone number. Their first move was to try telephoning, but there was no answer.

"Probably still at work," suggested Arthur, who was completely wrong.

"Or Tom's already been there, and done what he threatened," said Cianawyn, equally incorrectly.

The necessary paperwork for Arthur's release finally completed, they made their way out to the car park and their trusty station wagon. Cianawyn had to fight to restrain her impatience.

She was agitated by Tom Beaumaris' stated plans, and desperately wanted to stop him – to save him from himself, much more importantly than saving Trevor Salmon. But she could see how unsteady on his feet Arthur was. 'He really shouldn't be doing this,' she thought, but loved him for insisting on making the effort to support her. There was no point in trying to hurry him, he was already doing his best.

In more time than she wanted, but less time than it really should have taken, they found their way out to the Dunes.

Under other circumstances, they'd have made a leisurely sight-seeing drive of it. On the fringe of Dunbar, as close to coast as the name implied, the area had long been favoured by the well-to-do, such as the earlier generations of the Salmon family. Ostensibly 'holiday homes' and 'beach houses', many of the residences still retained a certain grandeur. Well-maintained timber gables, iron-laced verandahs, doors and windows still picked out with stained glass features reflecting the local flora and fauna – all contributed to a strong sense that "here be money, and plenty of it".

Any such musings didn't occur to Cianawyn and Arthur this time, though.

After a wrong turn or two, the Dunes being too old to have been laid out in a conventional grid pattern, Cianawyn drew their station wagon up outside the Salmons' address. There was a surprisingly similar vehicle already parked in the driveway.

"Tom's car?" asked Arthur.

"I don't think so," his beloved replied. "I've only ever seen him driving that old green sedan." She paused, her fingers on the doorhandle. "This is a silly time to think of it, but I realize now that I should have called the police and told them what was going on," she said.

Arthur shrugged. "You'd have been dropping Tom right into trouble, and I thought the idea was to keep him out of it. Stop him before anything happened."

"Ye-e-e-s," she said carefully, "I'm more worried about Trevor Salmon, to be honest. One of his thugs has already put you in the hospital, remember."

"Catch me once, shame on you. Catch me twice, shame on me," he replied coldly.

"You've already said that you're not up to a fight."

"I can dodge what I see coming."

"Even a bullet? We're talking about a serious criminal."

Arthur shrugged again. "We can play innocent. We're on his side. Heard about the threat and came to warn him."

"It might work," Cian admitted.

Putting on an air of confidence that neither of them truly felt, the couple walked up the driveway, hand in hand. After taking a deep breath and squaring her shoulders, Cianawyn knocked on the door.

For a minute or two, there was no response. Then, just as their worried frowns were deepening, there was the rattle of a small chain and the door swung open. A small Asian woman in a stained t-shirt and jeans blinked up at them.

"You for Mister Salmon, too? Busy, busy, busy today! He's not here. Gone on holiday. I just cleaning up."

"We're not the first callers?" asked Cianawyn.

"Ah, phone go crazy. I not answer – that's what Mister Salmon told me. Man come earlier. I told him to go away. He did, but then come back."

Cianawyn gave a good, succinct description of Tom Beaumaris, and asked, "Was that the man?"

The woman nodded. "Think so. Said he wanted Mister Salmon urgently on business."

"I'll bet," muttered Arthur.

"I told him, boss on holiday. Not back for weeks he told me. Man get upset, want to know holidaying where."

"I'd like to know the same thing," admitted Cianawyn.

"I tell you what I told him. Gone to Bali, I think. Heard him say that on phone just after I arrived."

The couple exchanged vexed looks.

"I suppose there's a slim chance we might catch him at the airport," suggested Arthur.

"No, no. Not airport," said the cleaner. "Sailing. Mister Salmon, he got his own yacht," she said, with more than a hint of pride in her employer.

"Of course he does," said Cianawyn. "I've heard about it before."

"Righto," said Arthur. "Dunbar marina it is, then."

The little cleaning lady scoffed. "Hah! Mister Salmon not keep his yacht there! Too many people he don't like hang around there, he say. No, he keep boat off Sandy Beach, so he can look down off High Point."

'That would fit with what I hear of Trevor's character,' thought Cianawyn. 'Looking down on everybody.'

"He take little boat to beach, and go out to yacht. He took me once, for party – he's good boss. Looks after me."

"I'm sure that you're very useful to him," replied Cianawyn. "And loyal."

"You bet."

"Did you tell Tom – the other man who was here – about the yacht?" asked Arthur.

"Yes... he said he had something to give Mister Salmon. I said to wait till he got back, but man said it very important. Matter of life and death he told me. He seemed very serious, so I told him. Don't know how he think he'll get out to yacht, but not my problem."

Thanking the chatty housekeeper for her help, the couple made their way back to their wagon.

"Okay, I'm going to call the police and let them know what's going on," declared Cianawyn.

"Insofar as we actually know ourselves," cautioned her husband.

"True, but I know enough to be concerned, and to think that you and I might need some back-up."

Cianawyn pulled out her mobile phone and dialled the Dunbar Police Station. Unfortunately, her call was answered by Constable Nicholas. This was problematic on a couple of counts: Nicholas was even more misogynistic than D.S. Sterling and tended to regard complaints from women as not worth his time – frivolous or over-reacting, most of them, was his attitude. Further, he'd had to deal with Cianawyn Lauder before, and he'd come out on the wrong end of things, which only increased his resistance to taking her report seriously.

"Look, just put me through to the detectives, please," she said, with some asperity.

"Mister Sterling is busy," Nicholas lied.

"Fine. Let me talk to Detective Mulholland."

"The Detective Sergeant is in charge," was the unhelpful reply.

"You just told me that he's busy!"

"He is."

"Then put me through to the other detective, please," Cianawyn said through clenched teeth.

"Mister Sterling insists that calls go to him." This wasn't strictly true, but was a good deflection, as far as the constable was concerned. "I've made a note of what you've said, and I'll pass it on to him."

"Urgently, please!"

"Yeah, of course," said Nicholas, hanging up on the indignant woman before she could say anything more.

He did, indeed, write a note, condensing Cianawyn's detailed explanation of the situation down to: "Possible problem, Trevor Salmon's yacht, anchored off Sandy Beach?"

The scribbled message was dropped casually into Sterling's In-Tray while the Detective Sergeant was making himself another terrible coffee. It was purely by chance that Rita Mulholland saw it before her boss. She'd been coming back from her own desk to report her lack of success at locating or contacting Trevor Salmon, and when she saw that man's name on the top of the wire basket, her eyes lit up.

She turned just as Sterling returned, and waved the note, "I don't believe it! A lead!"

Bob looked quizzical, waiting for Rita to explain.

"I've been getting nowhere in trying to find Trevor Salmon – I assume you've had no more success, or you'd have told me," she said.

"Of course," the D.S. replied, although that may or may not have been true.

"This note was on top of your In basket."

The two detectives looked over the scrap of paper.

"That's Nicholas' writing," observed Mulholland.

"Scrawl like that, he should be a doctor, not a copper," muttered Sterling. "Ask him what the hell it's supposed to mean."

When questioned, the surly constable gave a curt, barely useful summation of Cianawyn's call. Someone – he hadn't caught who – was 'out to get' Trevor Salmon, who was apparently on his yacht, moored off Sandy Beach.

"It sounds as though we'd better get over there," said Mulholland.

The Detective Sergeant frowned. Like Nicholas, he'd had dealings with Cianawyn Lauder before, and hadn't enjoyed the experience.

"You go," he replied. "Call me if there's anything to it. I'll wait here. See if a better lead turns up."

Rita gritted her teeth. She knew from experience that there was no point in arguing. She had a considerably higher opinion of Ms Lauder's value as a source of information. Well, if there was anything to the report, she'd soon find out.

Setting out for the same destination, but with rather less distance to travel than the detective, Cianawyn and her beau had their own misgivings.

"Any idea of how we'll get out to this yacht?" asked Arthur.

"No. I'm hoping we won't need to, if I'm honest. Fingers crossed, Tom will be as stumped as us."

Alas, that was not the case. When the housekeeper had provided the information of Salmon's whereabouts, the teacher had thanked her graciously, then driven away with no apparent haste. Two blocks away, he'd pulled his car over to the side of the road and sat, deep in thought, for some moments.

His mission sharpened his already quick mind. Very soon, he'd had a flash of inspiration. He drove back into Dunbar, to the school he knew so well. Once into the school grounds, he made his way to the storage shed where most of the larger sports equipment was kept.

He hadn't had much to do with Physical Education classes for a few years. The days when all academic staff were expected to do 'double duty' as sports coaches were, thankfully, past, although several still took on such roles by choice.

His master key, as he'd hoped, allowed him access through the shed's side door. Tom looked around and smiled. Yes, they were still there. A few single-scull kayaks, from when Dunbar High had actively pursued rowing as a sport of choice, and Beaumaris had been an enthusiastic instructor. He patted the hull of one, then opened the large roller door at the front of the shed.

He slung a coil of rope over his shoulder, then perched the boat on top of that. Propping the scull against an outside wall, Tom meticulously closed the roller door from the inside, tidied the shed to make his actions less obvious, and locked up after himself. Then he carried the craft to his car.

There was an old blanket on the back seat, which had been used for impromptu picnics with his wife and son – memories that brought a wistful smile to his face, even as he laid the blanket across the roof of the car. Just in case he _did_ survive this enterprise, he thought, it would be good to not damage the paintwork. Tom Beaumaris had a very tidy mind.

He lifted the kayak onto the blanket, opened the windows of all four doors, and tied the little boat down tightly. He clambered in through the driver's window, and raised all four windows enough to secure the rope. Calmly, he drove back out of the school grounds and set off for Sandy Beach.

Sandy Beach. High Point. Deep Creek. Some of the place names around the district were woefully unimaginative, Tom mused as he drove. It seemed as though, in pioneering days, nothing happened that was memorable enough to be preserved on the maps being prepared at the time. Not like other places in Australia that he'd heard of. Places like Murdering Hut Creek, or Dead Man's Beach. He chuckled to himself as he pondered, at some point in the future, Sandy Beach being rechristened as something more colourful.

Vengeance Beach. Retribution Cove. He patted the package on the passenger seat beside him. Exploding Yacht Bay – that had a satisfying ring to it.

.000.

31

———————

The motion of the yacht bobbing at anchor bothered Jonah Latukefu slightly. He'd been aboard before, as Trevor's guest at a few parties, but this time he didn't have the distractions of scantily clad girls, or a copious quantity of alcohol. Oh, sure, he had a can of beer in his hand, and he'd been assured that there was plenty more available, but he was still uneasy.

The Lofton brothers had collected him and whisked him to the boat very quickly – too quickly for comfort, now he reflected on it. He couldn't find his phone, unaware that nimble-fingered Jonny had removed it while Josh was first conversing with Trevor.

That conversation was a big part of the unease. It had seemed cordial enough. Very positive, even, with Jonah being invited to take on a significant role in the lucrative business that Salmon controlled. Latukefu knew what that business was – he'd been a customer for some time, after all. He had no misgivings about bringing anyone else into the same web.

In truth, Trevor <u>was</u> considering putting Jonah into the role suddenly vacated by the carelessly-arrested Graham Mount. The footballer was big enough to look threatening. A couple of weeks at sea might determine if he was stable and reliable enough to be trusted. Otherwise, the Pacific offered plenty of hungry predators as a 'clean-up' crew.

Perhaps Jonah had some instinctive awareness of that possibility as he looked out over a rail at the lapping ocean water. He jumped as a hand was laid on his shoulder. Deck shoes were quiet, and he hadn't heard Ronny's approach.

"You okay, mate?" Ronny asked.

"Yeah. Yeah, I guess so. Lot to take in, that's all," the islander replied.

"Of course, mate. All the more reason to relax and enjoy the holiday."

"How come we're just sitting out here? Are we waiting for someone else?"

Ronny had wondered that himself, thinking that perhaps Trevor had some plan to get Graham released and have him join them. But the boss had dismissed that out of hand. The big man was expendable. Unreliable, and easily discredited as a witness if necessary. Discredited or disposed of.

No, the reason for the delay was simply some annoyingly inconvenient weather conditions. Wind and current running against them. The motor yacht could prevail against them, if required, but Salmon saw insufficient urgency to waste fuel, when a little patience would see the wind turn and allow them to sail away easily.

Lofton relayed this explanation to his new shipmate, who seemed content with the answer.

"Ronny, you've been... involved in this business for a while, haven't you?"

The smaller man shrugged. "I guess so, yeah. Have you got doubts about it? I can tell you, the money's good. The boss looks after us."

"I guess that's what was bothering me. I don't know Mister Salmon very well."

"He'll treat you as you treat him. Play him straight, and you'll be right. Crossing him isn't a good idea, but there's no reason why you should."

Lofton was clearly sincere in his assessment, and Jonah was

reassured.

"Is it the business itself you've got doubts about?" Ronny asked.

Latukefu shook his head. "Nah, that doesn't bother me. Just cos I study law, doesn't mean I'm committed to it, eh? As long as I'm looked after, I'll be okay."

Lofton smiled and said, "You'll be looked after alright. My brother's down below right now, helping Darryl set up to make more Major Happy."

Jonah was satisfied. It was clear he had no moral objections to helping bring anyone else onto the same pharmaceutical path that he now travelled. Just as long as he was taken care of.

Looking out to sea, neither Jonah nor Ronny could see a green sedan pull into the small car park at Sandy Beach. Even if they'd noticed it, there was little chance of either paying it any attention. Neither would have recognised the vehicle.

With casual but brisk efficiency, Tom untied his securing rope and took the kayak from the roof. He carried the small craft down to the beach, and laid it on the sand just above the water's edge. He quickly went back to the car, extracted the paddle from the back seat, and the package from the front. With a satisfied smile, he locked the car and made his way back to the scull.

The beach wasn't quite deserted, but none of the handful of joggers and dog walkers were close enough to notice that the man pushing the kayak out into the waves, before climbing into it, wasn't really dressed for the exercise.

It had been quite a while since Tom had rowed, and he struggled with the surf at first. But before long, muscle memory kicked in (aided by sheer bloody-minded determination) and he made his way out past the breakers. Never taking his eyes off his objective, he paddled on steadily, those on the yacht unaware of his approach.

He'd only just passed the line of the breakers when Cianawyn and Arthur pulled up in the carpark, alongside the green sedan. Looking out, they saw the small craft on the far side of the waves, and rightly assumed that it was Tom.

"That's that," said Arthur. "Nothing we can do now."

His wife nodded unhappily. "Nothing but wait for the police. Whatever happens next, they'll have to deal with it. At least, whatever happens to Tom, Trevor Salmon should get <u>some</u> sort of come-uppance."

"I guess so. I certainly hope so, at any rate," said Arthur as he reached into the pocket of the door beside him, and extracted a small but powerful pair of binoculars. They were kept in the car for use on whale- and dolphin-watching occasions with Callie.

Chivalrously, he handed them to his darling bride. With a grateful smile, Cianawyn looked out at the scull, and confirmed, "Yes, that's definitely Tom."

She kept the field glasses fixed on the figure ploughing resolutely out to the bigger boat. Consequently, she was much more aware of Beaumaris' progress than anyone on board his target.

Ronny and Jonah were still leaning on a rail, looking out to sea. Below decks, Darryl had almost finished setting up his makeshift laboratory. Jonny Lofton was still being prevailed upon to hold and move the heavier items. He wasn't as strong as Graham Mount, but he was strong enough, and smarter than his predecessor as Frankem's assistant. In the wheelhouse, Trevor was engrossed in navigation charts. When he did glance up, it was only to look at the sky to judge the prevailing wind by cloud movement.

Only Cianawyn knew that Tom had managed to bring his kayak right alongside the yacht. A small rolling swell brought the two hulls into contact. Of those on the yacht, only Salmon noticed the thud. By far the most experienced sailor aboard, he had an immediate sense that something was wrong. He looked out on all sides, but could see nothing amiss. The kayak sat so close to the waterline that, right beside the yacht's hull, it was below the line of Trevor's sight.

Beaumaris retrieved his perilous package from between his feet, and quickly removed the thick fabric swaddling that had ben protecting it. What was revealed was a smaller parcel, wrapped in a couple of sheets of newspaper. The core of the package was a stoppered beaker of thin glass, in which was a very carefully concocted compound of chemicals.

It was a formula which Tom had never shared with his students, for the sound reason that it produced something as unstable as it was dangerous. Some chemistry teachers, he knew, enjoyed 'showing off' to their pupils by crafting tiny amounts of a somewhat safer variant that still produced a spectacular display of sound and light when triggered correctly. Beaumaris' view, though, was that a little of such knowledge was a very dangerous thing. Especially so when entrusted to inquisitive young minds who may thirst to experiment. What nestled in his lap was a powerful explosive which must <u>not</u> be handled carelessly.

There was nothing careless about Tom's preparation, though. Even the newspaper had been chosen with deliberation, for symbolic, not scientific reasons. Only the bomb maker himself would ever appreciate it, he expected, but the outer layer contained an article about the retirement of a veteran football coach. It had been folded and wrapped so that some of the headline stood out: "It's All Over At Last".

Following his instincts, Trevor had come onto the deck to investigate the noise that he'd heard. He first approached Ronnie and Jonah. They'd noticed nothing, but dutifully followed their boss as he made his way around the vessel.

Even through her binoculars, Cianawyn couldn't make out the small, satisfied nod made by the bereaved teacher, but she did see the movement of his arm as he lobbed his package up onto the deck of the yacht, and his effort to paddle quickly away.

Trevor and his two men saw the parcel suddenly appear from over the side. Jonah rushed over to the landward railing and saw the kayak turning away.

"Hey, you!" he called, to no response.

Alerted by the sound of breaking glass as the thing landed, Trevor began to back away. It was Ronny Lofton who stepped forward and saw a dark stain spreading across the newspaper, as some sort of liquid seeped out of the broken beaker.

He just had time to register the word "Over" before the chemical responded to the air, and flared brilliantly. The dazzle lasted only a moment before the rest of the potent mixture was triggered.

Down in the drug lab, Darryl and Jonny died without even knowing what happened. So too did Jonah, his back to the explosion. Trevor Salmon saw his fate, but only for a split second. His death was quicker than his brother's, Solomona's, or those of Laura and Ted Beaumaris.

It was the faces of Laura and Ted that shone in Tom's mind's eye, even as a flying fragment of the yacht's hull hit the back of his skull, and he joined his loved ones in death.

Ashore, Cianawyn turned her head at the critical instant, too late to warn Arthur to close his eyes. He was momentarily blinded, but recovered quickly enough to see debris raining down through a cloud of smoke. A little closer to shore, the kayak bobbed upside down on the water disturbed by the blast. Evidently cracked, it sank quickly, with no sign of its occupant.

Variously sized pieces of flotsam were all that remained of the yacht. A few of them had fallen coastward, and were already being picked up by the surf and borne to the beach.

"Well, I suppose that stuff will be evidence, of a sort," said Rita Mulholland, getting out of the car that had just pulled in beside the wagon.

Cianawyn and Arthur stood by the detective, and all three stared out at the floating mess.

"You got my message, then?" said Lauder.

"Such as it was. I don't know exactly what you told Constable Nicholas, but I received just enough to get me here."

Cianawyn started to explain details, but Rita held up her hand.

"I've a feeling you'd best not say too much, Ms Lauder. If I have questions, I'll ask them, I assure you."

Grimly, Arthur asked, "What about your boss? Will he feel the same?"

"Detective Sergeant Sterling chose not to respond to your call himself. Instead he despatched me. So, he saw even less than I did. He saw nothing at all," was the even-toned response.

"And you?" asked Cianawyn quietly.

The detective shrugged. "I saw nothing that I could consider as evidence. As I pulled into the car park I saw an explosion some way off shore, which I've learned was the yacht I came here to see. The only witnesses were sightseers at the beach, who could only tell me that there was no indication of another sailing or motor vessel near the scene. Correct so far?"

"Well, yes, but..."

"Please, Mr. Bayer. I understand you've just come out of hospital. I imagine you're not – at your best. Probably wisest if you say nothing."

Arthur didn't argue. He knew that the detective had a sharp mind. Mulholland turned to his wife.

"Ms Lauder, the report I got from Constable Nicholas was, let's say, light on detail. I understand that you had some information of an unspecified threat made to Trevor Salmon, and that you were subsequently made aware that Mister Salmon was aboard his yacht, in this vicinity."

"Yes, that's what his housekeeper told us," confirmed Cianawyn.

"But this housekeeper knew nothing of the threat?"

"No, she –"

"I think 'No' is enough. It was good of you, as a concerned citizen, to contact us, as well as trying to alert Salmon directly. I take it that the exact nature of this threat was a mystery to you."

"Er... yes..." Cianawyn conceded.

"And the person making the threat, did they make themselves known to you here?"

"Not as such, no..."

"So, you couldn't confirm their presence here at the scene, nor if they had any involvement in the explosion I saw as I arrived?"

"I certainly couldn't," chimed in Arthur.

It was technically true. He hadn't looked through the binoculars, and the green car could have belonged to – well – <u>anybody</u> who owned a green car. His beloved was less sure, and that uncertainty showed on her face.

Mulholland gazed out to sea for a moment, then quietly said, "I'm going down to the beach, to see what, if anything, has washed ashore. Can I suggest that the two of you have a little chat?"

After the detective had walked away, Cianawyn turned to her husband and asked, "What do we say? Tell her everything about Tom?"

"What everything, darling? Tom was grieving, he made a threat. We followed him here, sure, but we don't know if he carried through on it."

"Oh, come on, Ay – the explosion..."

"May have had nothing to do with him. Pure chance. We could even say we don't know if he got here..."

Cianawyn pointed to the green car. "The police will identify that, quickly enough. And I know he rowed out there."

"But we don't know what happened. Sweetheart, I never knew Tom as well as you did, but I liked the guy. And Lord knows, he had a damned good reason to want to get revenge on Salmon."

"But we can't know where it might end. What if Tom becomes a vigilante? If you can kill once, it becomes easier to kill again. Remember Bronwyn Fox?"

Arthur nodded, remembering a woman who'd become a multiple murderer.

"But there has to be a <u>reason</u>," he said. "You told me – Tom's whole reason was his wife and son. With them gone..."

"I suppose so."

"Even on the remote chance that Tom survived, I wouldn't be keen to hand him over to the coppers. Mulholland's alright, but her boss would want to big-note himself somehow." Arthur had a long-standing negative opinion of police in general, and although recent experience had offered up a few exceptions, D. S. Sterling was very much of the type to reinforce his cynicism.

"Whether or not he <u>did</u> survive, there will be questions asked. If they can somehow prove the blast was his fault, there has to be justice," said Cianawyn, more firmly than she felt.

"On behalf of Trevor Salmon? You're kidding!" scoffed Arthur. "I think <u>that</u> is where the justice has been done, given what seem to have been Salmon's real business activities."

Cianawyn was silent for some moments, before replying, "I can't argue with that. And we really aren't certain of very much, when I think about it. Okay, I won't lie to the detective, but I won't make any suggestions or suppositions, either."

Neither said anything more. They held hands and walked to the beach. Rita was at the waterline, kneeling to examine some of the material washing ashore.

Without looking up at them, she said, "You know, I wouldn't be surprised if we manage to recover just enough evidence to suggest that there was a drug lab on board, and the explosion had something to do with that."

"Really?" said Cianawyn, as mildly as she could.

"We've recently received very strong evidence that Trevor Salmon was involved in the manufacture and distribution of drugs. I was about to go looking for him myself when your message came into the station – happy coincidence, that one."

"My message, yes. Detective Mulholland, the man who made the threat was Tom Beaumaris – please, let me finish," she said as Rita held up her hand. "I know Tom was very upset by the loss of his family, but he gave me no specific details of anything he intended. I know he was here at the beach, and I know he paddled out to that yacht. I don't know if he was even able to speak to Salmon, far less confront him or do anything else."

"I see. It's entirely possible, then, that Mister Beaumaris had the terrible misfortune to have been in the exact wrong place when the floating laboratory came to grief."

Arthur nodded in satisfaction. "Entirely possible, I'd say. Terribly tragic, after his wife and son were killed, but perhaps that's closure, of a sort."

"There's a lot to be said for closure," agreed Rita, quietly.

.ooo.

32

Sunday afternoon was still rehearsal time for *Sweeney Todd, The Musical* at the Terrence Community Theatre, even or perhaps especially with a little more than two weeks until opening. The litany of misfortune and drama that had befallen the show would have been enough to cause most directors – amateur or professional – to have given up in despair.

In truth, Shauna Shallacot had very nearly done so, but she hated to admit defeat. Fortunately, her musical director, Dolly Bertram, was similarly resilient. Dolly determinedly looked for something positive in almost any situation.

The pair of them had received, and made, numerous phone calls over the preceding two days, especially in this morning's hours. Remarkably, *The Musical* was once more fully cast.

"Even better, this lot, ducks!" Dolly had enthused.

The director may not have quite shared that level of enthusiasm, but she had to admit that things had worked out better than she'd expected. The leading roles were as intact as they'd been for a few weeks now, and several smaller roles had been swapped around and recast.

It was <u>not</u>, as she'd feared, 'shuffling the deckchairs on the Titanic'. The sudden loss of Darryl Frankem had brought her close to giving up, but almost immediately afterwards she'd gotten an unexpected call from Gordon Teller.

Gordon had just been permanently appointed as CRD-FM's breakfast announcer (well, as permanent as such a job can ever be) and he was offering to promote the show on-air, as a favour to his friends Arthur and Cianawyn. Arthur's role as Colonel Jeffrey wasn't physically demanding, so he'd be able to remove both his sling and soft collar before going on stage, without much risk of further damage. Cianawyn, who by now knew more of the lines than she'd realised, had already taken on Mary Fletcher's role capably. Intuitively feeding Gordon's ego, Shauna had convinced him to join his friends on-stage, taking on the madhouse keeper's role vacated by the much-missed Tom Beaumaris.

There was a certain prestige in having a prominent radio personality in the cast, as well as obvious promotional advantages. Gordon would be a very different man to work with than Mike Salmon had been, but that was no bad thing in Shauna's view.

Frankem's role as Jasper, patriarch of the Oakley clan, had gone to young Nick Rankin. He was decades younger than ideal, but a fake beard and a hitherto-unrevealed flair as a character actor would let them get away with it. Shauna would have liked to cast their other new recruit as Jasper, but he was adamant that that, given the timeframe, he could and would only commit to memorizing fewer lines. And, she had to admit, the character of Judge Brandon was given considerable authority by the retired police officer, Kenneth Derbishire.

Kenneth had made the mistake of remarking, over a few drinks, that he "hadn't been on stage since High School". His reluctance to return to the acting fold couldn't withstand the combined efforts of Dolly, Cianawyn, and Arthur, especially when Callie had gotten behind the collective push.

The dress rehearsal was mere minutes from starting when Cianawyn's phone rang. Adeline Bond glared, but the Stage Manager had lost some cachet with the Players when she'd tried to refuse to allow any of 'her' crew to fill in on-stage roles. The Wardrobe Mistress had openly defied that instruction, recognizing the troupe's plight. As it happened, Cianawyn had just been reaching to turn off her phone (normal backstage etiquette) when it rang. It was only because the Caller ID showed Callie's name that it was even answered.

"Got to make it quick, Mum. Dress rehearsal's just about to start," Cianawyn said, waving a vague placatory hand towards Adeline.

"Oh, of course. Sorry, dear, but I did think I should share this with you, so you can share it with appropriate folks there. I've just had a call from Georgie Fletcher. Her show *Diskolos* opens at the Arcadium a week after your show closes. She's offered me a couple of tickets to the first night, as company for her parents. Would you care to join me? We could buy a ticket for Arthur, I'm sure."

With Callie stopping for breath, there was a chance for Cianawyn to reply. "That's wonderful, Mum. I think there might be a couple of other people here who'd like to attend too – maybe we can make a big celebration of it. I'll let everyone know. <u>After</u> this rehearsal. I'll call you back then, okay?"

As soon the line went dead, she switched the phone off. Spreading her arms helplessly to Adeline, she said, "Sorry Adeline. I guess with so little positivity recently, Mum just felt that she had to tell me some good news about Georgie Fletcher."

"Oh! She's… alright, then? She was a good girl, as I remember her."

Cianawyn gave a very brief update, which mollified the irritable Stage Manager. Adeline was good-hearted, in her way, but had cultivated the brusque persona for a long time.

The news would be shared with the rest of the Dunbar and District Players soon enough. And yes, Dolly and a few others would be keen to make an excursion to Sydney for Georgie's Opening Night.

Outside, the sun was starting to break through the heavy clouds.

-xXx-

NEXT…

Cromwell House is supposed to be a safe, restful haven for older folks who can't, or don't want to, look after themselves any more.

Death may be inevitable, but it's meant to be peaceful.

When sudden violence and very un-peaceful death happen, Cianawyn and her mother are naturally worried. Was it a moment of madness, or is there something even more dangerous going on?

CHARLES ROYLE THROWN - A Golden Gardens Mystery

ACKNOWLEDGMENTS

First and foremost, I have to thank my wife Meredith, and her mother Maggie. Golden Gardens wouldn't exist without them, and their ideas and encouragement continue to keep me going.

There are a few other people nearby who've contributed advice and support, too. Carole and David, Sue and Greg, Julie and Roger, and Margaret - thank you all.

And a huge thanks to my old friend David Davies (has it really been that many years? Wow!) Dave is a very fine artist, and is responsible for this book's striking cover.

ABOUT THE AUTHOR

RENOIR has turned his hand to a lot of jobs over the years, some more successfully than others. Full-time and pert-time, paid and voluntary. He's also travelled extensively, around Australia and across the world.

But he's adamant that experience is only valuable if you learn from it. Now he applies that experience to his writing, using it to nourish the plethora of stories that swirl in his head.

He lives in the Northern Rivers region of New South Wales, Australia. He shares his home with his darling bride, his trusty laptop, lots of books, and three eccentric cats who really run the household.

ALSO BY RENOIR

Find us at www.meredian.com.au

The DUBIOUS MAGIC Series:

The Wizard of Waramanga

The Carvings of Cobbemarmoo

The Mad Machines of Mundara

The Warriors of Wiwo'ole

The Spirits of Sron Dubh

The Sailors of Svalgsay

The Treasure of Tepatamwa

The Masks of Manovalo

ALSO:

The Fall of De Wilde - a Golden Gardens Mystery

Hall of the Mountain King (play)

The LOST Saga

He Was Beeb When I Knew Him

Mixed Blood